Thirteen Jewels of Transformation

Nalini MacNab

Copyright © 2024 Nalini MacNab

All rights reserved

ISBN-13: 978-0-9993198-6-4

Cover design by: Joan Weisman, with a portion of the image created by DALL-E
Printed in the United States of America

Contents

Introduction

Solstice, December 2022

The Solstice alignment was a massive re-set. I felt it in my bones, as the saying goes. It was as though the frequencies of the Earth heaved upwards all at once. A set of intense adjustments began to move throughout the surface world and within each of its inhabitants.

Vision came easily as I looked at lines of light laced through a turbulent 2023. Every aspect of the passage of the coming year would be a rarity of cosmic proportions. I was excited, anticipating what looked like tsunami-level shifts in consciousness. Would crust displacement follow? Would Gaia's surface world physically move?

The Earth is well within the turning of a Great Cycle. Astrologers agree, and that is saying something. Yes, there are astrological alignments that repeat within our lifetimes. Not like this, though. Not like this. Bombarded with quantum field information from the more recently discovered Kuiper Belt Objects / Trans-Neptunian Objects / Dwarf Planets, our world is flooded with streaming cosmic consciousness. What a gift Gaia's transition is.

The Earth is inviting in an upgrade of her baseline energies, like an operating system upgrade, only more potent. As this occurs, many lower vibrations, like hate, terror, and war, will fade away, as those energies will no longer be supported here. It's like feeding a high-performance car premium fuel. It just can't digest 'regular' anymore. The 'digestion' issues run both ways, of course. You can't put lower octane fuel in a high-performance vehicle and expect it to run well, and premium in an older model is an inefficient use of energy that can burn out the engine. This calendar year is a passage of adjusting to higher frequency.

With the constantly shifting patterns on the planet, forward-seeing or prophecy of any kind seemed pointless. The moment something is seen, its value lies only in that moment. Everything can and will change in an hour, a day, a week, who knows? Even so, as I sat down to meditate, my awareness was shown a passage ahead.

In my vision, I saw the year 2023 spiraling out in linear time like a strand of cosmic DNA. The spiral broadened as my vision took me deeper. Within its depths glowed what looked like a strand of precious jewels, each surrounded by golden light.

The voice of the Great Mother informed me that these illuminated orbs are precious gems of transmission from Her heart. Each infusion of divine love carries new frequencies and higher octaves of what is needed to build a world as a fresh expression of reality.

Each jewel in this cosmic passage of rebirth represented a full moon. For example, the wolf moon of 6th January showed up at 16 degrees of Cancer. This energy initiated a cycle of deep, deep nurturing. It is a cycle that will amplify through the full moon of 26th December, also in the sign of Cancer. Gaia moves through a transformational passage of what it is to nurture and be nurtured by the Divine in us all.

The first few full moons of 2023 occur at 16 degrees of their respective signs. Sixteen, in the Major Arcana of the Tarot, the Tower card. The energies of this archetype are an initiation into letting go of Identities whose time has come to dissolve. The story of the Fool relates the experience of seeing an edifice the ego has built, and watching it be struck by lightning and crumble. Expressions of doing and being that cannot thrive in higher energy frequencies will cease to exist. Regardless of the degree of sign for each lunar alignment, each full moon in this cycle holds a profound initiation.

This strand of cosmic jewels is a whole. Each gem builds upon the last, infusing Gaia's electromagnetic field with higher frequencies and energetic building blocks of being. These elements of divine design are forms of Universal nurturing. Our universe is up-shifting, and we are shifting with her, ready or not.

As I contemplated this vision and its 13 jewels, the Hathors, the celestial beings, not the Egyptian Goddess, made themselves known. To say it had been a while would be an understatement. I recalled the infusions of ancient Egypt and had been aware of Hathor presence through my transmissions from time to time. But, while the Hathors' energies are unmistakable, I still wondered if this was part of the more significant global infusion or something I was seeing for my personal comprehension.

I was impulsed to look at Tom Kenyon's book, "The Hathor Material." The book opened to the About section, and there, on the second page, was the sentence, "The Hathors originally gave me the entire body of information in a stream of thirteen unbroken chapters." Thirteen! Cosmic laughter ensued. Grateful tears filled my eyes. Validation arrives when we least expect it and, sometimes, when we need it most. This passage is going to be wondrous!

How does Source's divine nurturing feel? What does it feel like within your Source Essence? Within this transit, we will all begin to know.

The lovely lunar rabbit year provides gentle, sustainable support for these infusions and transformations. In Chinese astrology, the rabbit represents peace, prosperity, and longevity, keywords for emerging abundance.

How auspicious that a Rabbit Year supports this passage of receiving Thirteen Jewels of Transformation.

Magic and mystery embraced me as I sat with what was about to unfold. The story began to write itself, like a tale told long ago.

Once upon a time, Gaia moved through a passage that had never been seen nor experienced in a so-called physical world. Thirteen moons marked its trajectory.

Many would see, feel, and know this passage. Thirteen Jewels of Transformation is one woman's story.

January

The Pearl ~ Initiation of New Light

*I*t is time.

The voice of Source, Spirit, God/Goddess/All That Is, the zero-point field, cosmic consciousness, or whatever definitions one wanted to give that voice, rang through her being.

"I hear you. I am listening. I am ready." She folded her legs and settled in to meditate.

Cosmic laughter followed her into the Silence.

Fitting in was not something she was here to do. She tried, really she did; sometimes successfully, sometimes not. And yet, she had to learn about this world because it was soon to enter a radical transition. And she had chosen to bring something special to the collective consciousness of the planet, no, something extraordinary. She knew that she had to seed this awareness and help it to grow in fresh, cosmically fertilized soil.

She and the planet had many heart-to-hearts about what was to come. The woman knew she would have to wait, learn a new kind of patience, and open her heart to limits she had never recognized or encountered before. Her quest took her to many places and into many people's lives until one day, she remembered her why and her inner journey took over. She thought she had embodied this alignment many years ago, but now, limits she had not known existed began to dissolve. She had been living in fragile boxes, in transparent containers with invisible constructs and constraints. Her every intention was to dissolve them all.

Sitting with her eyes closed in meditation, she saw a string of jewels threading through the coming year. Thirteen full moons, she remembered. What is it about thirteen orbs of light? As each appeared to her inner sight, she noticed filaments of golden light connecting them all, merging into a single thread. So finely was this web woven that a single connection was all she could perceive.

Each orb shone with a unique light, quality, and color. Some seemed to be in the form of jewels she recognized, but upon closer observation, those images disappeared. Each orb held specific frequencies of sound and vibration. Her level of awe grew with each breath as she continued to observe and listen. The thread connecting the spheres was of the purest gold, exquisite in its clarity. She knew she was seeing a chain of precise and interlocking downloads. Tears of joy spoke to the feeling that she had never seen anything so beautiful. "Finally!" resounded through her entire being. How exquisite!

She wondered somewhere on the edge of awareness, "Why do I feel 'finally' when this is brand new?" The first and last images came together as though joined by a clasp. Then, all imagery dissolved into stillness.

The woman knew she had perceived the truth. She knew she had been called to bear witness. So, she looked into the lunar calendar's upcoming 'Water Rabbit' year to comprehend its significance.

The threads of thirteen jewels, orbs of quantum potential that each being would integrate in their own way, flowed within her inner waters. "This will change everything," she whispered to the stars. "This passage is not only a game changer but will change all the games of this world."

There is so much we do not know! And this is a new beginning. The woman began to allow the strand of transformative jewels to shape her vision. "Guide me," she requested. "Show me the way."

The upcoming full moon in the first week of January was less than a month away. She felt a strategy was needed. Was there a special place from which she could best perceive and receive? In stillness, she waited. And then, the answer came.

Point Lobos would be perfect for viewing the wolf moon, inner impulses insisted. And so, she made the journey. It was a long drive, whose one saving grace was several hours spent traveling the California coast. I'm glad this coast is still here, she thought. So beautiful! She thanked the cliffs, powerful cypress trees, sky and sea for being present for a new beginning.

Long ago, she had discovered this special place, this trinity of powerful forces. Perhaps it had found her. She had never been sure. It was a perfectly balanced nexus of earth, sky, and sea, perched on the edge of a continent, surrounded more by nature than the things of humankind.

The small peninsula was triangular in shape, surrounded by the sea on two sides, one of which hosted deep kelp beds. A tribe of sea otters populated the bay formed by the protective peninsula and could frequently be seen sunbathing or breaking open mollusks as they floated among the kelp. A slight clack-clacking of breaking shells added to the music of moving waves and soaring sea birds. It has been a long time, she thought as she hiked from her car to the edge of the sea.

Salt air and the smell of damp earth greeted her as she
maneuvered her body into the small cave, weathered into the
point of her favorite promontory. A natural geode, the boulder in
which she sat had split and shifted over the years to expose its
hollow center. Large enough to hold her body, the cavity lay
utterly hidden from the trail behind. She had sat here how many
times? She had no idea. This was her getaway, her gateway to
Infinite knowing. Here, embraced by the elements, she could let
down her guard and perceive.

As her back nestled into the wall of the tiny enclosure, she felt her
body shift in harmony with elemental forces. Her muscles relaxed
as her cells opened to what she was about to receive. Pounding
waves echoed against the cliff, rocking her gently with each surge.
Then, as the sun set, the moon rising with it, she opened her eyes
and her heart to ripples of light caressing the calming seas. Gazing
at the light on the water, she opened her inner sight.

It had been so long since she had felt this excitement, this joy, or
perhaps it only seemed that way. What was time, after all? The
days and years always seemed to disappear in her little nook,
sheltered from the world and wind, embraced by what was about
to be.

As the moon continued to rise in the night sky, she watched,
breathless, as a new presence infused the world around her. Milky
white gentleness moved through and into the land, stones, stars,
and trees. Its subtle yet ferocious emanations soothed body and
mind. Like an invisible fog, it permeated the breath and being of
watchful nocturnal creatures and those fast asleep. She watched
in awe as birthing energies changed the moonlit world.

The full moon's disk floated above a vast bank of energy, gleaming
as a pearl through clear, dark skies. She lifted her hands, cupping

the glowing disk before her, cherishing its light as she felt cherished. She lifted tender lips to the light between cupped hands, her heart drinking in this nourishing elixir.

"What is nurturing?" she wondered as her heart opened wider and wider.

The unmistakable voice of Source rang through her awareness.

Listen. Learn. This alignment is an advent. It is an accelerated replacement of what needs healing with the frequencies of wholeness. Feel the difference in energy between what seems to need healing and what wholeness is. Wholeness is moving in to replace outdated patterns of the old cycle. You are becoming the pearlescent vibration of a new foundation.

The first gift of this passage is a Pearl. Consider how a Pearl forms. A little mollusk, generally ignored by humankind except as something to be consumed, produces something wondrous, something these humans hold as valuable and of great price.

A grain of sand, ocean floor debris, or something artificial externally seed a Pearl. A tiny nucleus enters the mollusk, which will either form a Pearl or sometimes die, depending on how the insertion happened. Is one form of Pearl better than another? Is one of you better than another? Consider the Pearl. There is an insertion into this invertebrate creature that some might not consider precious. Think of the delicate process by which this little gem, this beautiful consolidation of grace, forms.

The Pearl forms around a seeded irritant. So runs the consensus of human observation. But, from the perspective of wholeness, is that irritant a problem? On the contrary, its insertion causes the mollusk to secrete Nacre, which surrounds and embraces what has become a precious seed with beautiful layers of grace. Is that not what happens to you? Whether by conception or emotional, psychic, or physical injection, you accept seeding into re-alignment at many points in your life.

Like that Pearl, your sovereign journey is what you make of your inner alignment. Some Pearls are beautifully round or oval. Some are strange shapes and sizes and colors. Yet, each form is equally precious.

The vision expanded, taking her to places long ago and far away. She saw how the idea of a Pearl being precious began in China many ages ago. She watched as the enlightenment traditions of this world adopted the Pearl as a symbol of the wish-fulfilling jewel. The jewel of freed awareness, of inestimable value, formed unseen within the depths of the unconscious.

Adjusting her seat in the geode, she whispered aloud, "What if the little mollusk is not trying to get rid of an irritant but honoring a seed form growing from its core?"

Shivering a bit, with gooseflesh rising on her arms, she began to hear another voice. She gazed upward and listened to the transmission coming through the alignment of the sun and moon.

"I reflect a new seeding of accelerated wholeness, heightened intuition, and heightened sensitivity. These qualities must now be honored.

"Here you are, gazing at my reflected light. Let yourself immerse deeply. Yes, there is intensity, and there will be more throughout this transition. Still, the power does not need to be run from nor avidly embraced. It is a passage of energies like any wave.

"What are the currents that carry you? A new cycle has new ways of being. Gaia is learning."

The voice of the alignment continued. "Like the little mollusk, deep under the water, deep in Source's embrace, you must find a new way. Think of the diversity, the variety of these luminous beings that come from an unassuming little creature. Its rigid outer shell protects the softness inside. Look what it produces! That Pearl, once seeded, grows on its own without further intervention. Each layer contributes to a marvelous shape, size, and color. Each of these qualities is a frequency.

"As you take each new step, each breath, filled with Source-led frequencies, and honor the Source Essence you are, you become your most-needed new form, emerging from what most call the Unknown."

Source rounded out the transmission with a single concept.

This knowledge is a fundamental shift in values for the entire planet.

The woman rested within the embrace of new wisdom. She knew it would integrate in its own time. "How must I navigate this new construct of reality?" she asked herself, the cosmos, and the wonder. She felt planted in newly minted softness. She sensed her body feeling for roots and nourishment, unsure of these new surroundings.

Source's voice stilled her questioning mind.

You will not find nurturing or grounding through any old ways.

"The last Solstice promised a total re-set," she thought to herself. Then, she whispered to the Essence inside her, "You never disappoint."

The woman sighed as awareness returned to her body, now stiff and chilled from exposure. Stretching, she left the cave and stood to walk, vowing to honor her seeing and to share it with those who might understand and share in her joy.

Waves beneath the cliff path continued to pound against the stone, making the trek back to her vehicle challenging. She knew this path well, but everything seemed strange and weirdly foreign after what she had just experienced. Fumbling in a side pocket for her keys, she crossed from the dirt path to the parking area in a meditative state. At this late hour, only her vehicle remained. "Thank you," she sighed, "I need the space."

Plopping herself down on the front seat of her car, she closed her eyes to let the initiation find home in her body. She knew from long practice that hearing is not enough. New frequencies must be integrated at the cellular level, and her body sometimes resisted this process. She grabbed a thermos from the center console, letting the aroma and warmth of tea refresh her. Then, pulling a journal from her daypack, she let Source's transmission flow through her heart and hands onto the page and into the environment.

My vision is the first of thirteen initiations, she wrote. What an immense transfusion Gaia is receiving. We must ingest what is most precious about ourselves to blossom and flourish in this new garden. We must walk a unique reflection of more refined light. As we allow the perceptual shift this alignment offers, we transform.

This Pearl will not lose its radiance regardless of what might be projected onto or through it. "This radiance is what I came for," she whispered to the page. "And yet, this, too, is shifting. Will we ultimately embody a constant morph-in-place?"

Waves crashing against the cliff beneath her seemed to answer. "In nature, nothing stays the same."

Her hands fell quietly into her lap as deep ancestral memories took over. She envisioned herself in the Temple at Dendera in ancient Egypt. It was a place thrumming with energy, making many visitors dizzy.

Visiting the site in this life, she had found it foreign yet achingly familiar. It had unsettled her, creating heart palpitations and taking her breath away so that she had to move from the central area, the field generator, and allow her body to settle.

At that time, as she breathed into her body's reactive memories, she recalled the training that had, long ago in another life, prepared her body for melding with and becoming the djed, a pillar of resonance. Her other life body had been trained for this. This body, prepared through other practices, attempted to do what it knew in this life and what the memories of the temple required. Her body buzzed so that her hands were shaking. The dissonance in her field was causing her heart to palpitate. She breathed quietly and calmly, allowing her body to synchronize its frequencies.

As her body quieted, memories of the temple's true purpose settled her heart. She recalled infusions from the Hathors. An advanced galactic civilization, the Hathors assist creation by seeding luminosity into structures receptive to this light. Their initial incursion into humanity was via the Sirian star portal and the temples of Egypt. She knew this, beyond intellectually, from within her cellular makeup. Grateful for the recollection, she felt her body let go. Little did she know that her Great Remembering had begun.

The woman's name was Fírinne, a Celtic word for truth. She reached for the comforting warmth of her thermos, smiling at the Celtic symbols etched upon it. As she sipped tea in the moonlight, she recalled that visit to Dendera. The truth of her experience thrummed through her body. She could feel herself seated outside the temple, letting her nervous system relax and her memories awaken.

Fírinne felt a memory build itself around her, filling her field. She knew how to rest in vision, letting it guide her to what was needed. Her inner sight deepened as she consciously relaxed. An intensely gentle field of energy entered her body. She recognized this field of divine love and wisdom. She knew its warm, nurturing embrace, its soft, pinkish-white light, infused with a faint aura of spikenard and roses.

The Hathor civilization had long ago introduced infusions of purity and divine love into temples along the Nile to assist its mystery schools. Hieroglyphs in those temples still depict an architecture of love-oriented power meant to be fully embodied by initiates. Having only just walked past those hieroglyphs in this life, she remembered and was glad.

She remembered acting as a conduit to assist in transducing high frequencies of cosmic love from the stars into the temple structures, instructing those who practiced mystical arts at these places of power. Into the design of the systems of the Giza Plateau, the epochal record of Sep Tepi, a world view oriented to direct Source connection, the Hathors infused their frequencies.

Sitting in her car in this life, still bathed in moonlight, she wondered whether the Hathors were involved in this full moon infusion. If so, this was undoubtedly a higher octave of earlier transmissions. Was she fulfilling the same function as she had then?

Faint chimes of laughter and a whiff of spikenard and rose followed her question. "Of course."

Was this an affinity on her part? Was this Source's way of showing her a more profound truth? Was this a broader perspective on what was happening?

"My mind wants to run away with this," she chuckled, taking a deep breath. "I'll let the memory play through and see where it takes me."

Source's voice answered her, stilling all thought with one syllable.

YES.

Still curious, the woman pondered what she had received.

"I was taught to transit a portal by embodying its qualities. Must I become this transition, one step, one breath, one moment of luminosity at a time? How miraculous that this happens all at once because there is no time. On what will I focus? My heart knows the adage, 'what you focus on, you become.' Does this hold true in a new foundation of reality?"

Source's soothing currents flowed through her, quieting her mind.

Let yourself love the process that you are. Let yourself be that embodied empowerment. You remember. There is nothing to fear.

As she wrote, her heart grew lighter and lighter. These are courageous and sustainable frequencies of being. This pearlescent light is a new foundational construct, a space within which any of us who so choose can safely dream new dreams. More frequencies will enter this construct with each of the thirteen full moons of 2023.

These infusions obliterate what has gone before. They form a fresh field of creative energy with which to begin anew. Some people, places, and circumstances will assimilate these frequencies and shift accordingly. Some structures and configurations will cease to exist as they cannot thrive in higher frequencies.

This first gem, this pearlescent construct, will assist us with our total reconfiguration, a radical and complete shift of our alignments. It begins a thorough and unconditional shifting from the inside out. One's perspective shifts from the current, personally identified self to the Source-Self or Source's point of view.

The pearlescent construct is not an in-between but is born of them all. Every one of our in-betweens and the worlds they intersect with are shifting. The new construct is replacing, bit by glorious bit, what is open and willing to be replaced at any moment.

As these gems unfold and integrate within us, may we see, each in our own ways, with Source's eyes.

Finally, Fírinne felt herself becoming a Pearl of great price, though she had no idea what it meant or would be. Her story had shifted. She was no longer the woman she had been. She sent love to that woman and all those who had gone before.

The woman, if she could still call herself that, took a few more sips of tea and turned the key in the ignition. "I do want to embody truth," Fírinne thought as her car's engine hummed to life. Switching on the headlights, she put the engine in gear and ventured into a new world with the precise and caring attention of all she had absorbed.

February

An Infusion of Sapphire

Had it been a month already? February's infusion required an energy adjustment and a more northerly location close to the sea. The North Atlantic is cold in winter. Its coasts can feel desolate and forbidding. There would be fewer people than at other times, which made sense for what Fírinne was about to attempt. Intense energy currents flowed toward the shore, not only through the ley lines. The infusion was building. She felt the surging waters and welcoming coastline where she would most optimally be able to receive the infusion. Grinning in anticipation, she booked her flights.

She arrived, navigated the airport and collected the car she had reserved online. Darkness was falling, but it was only a short distance to the coast and she was familiar with the roads. She stopped, once, for groceries and firewood and reached her rather remote destination just in time for sunset.

Luckily for her, someone had turned on the gas in the little cottage, and a fire burned merrily in the fireplace. Living warmth contrasted with the bitter cold outside. A small heater in the bedroom faced the already turned-down bed, which looked buried under an avalanche of comforters.

Too exhausted for much else, Fírinne banked the living room fire, turned down the bedroom heater and crawled in for the night, pausing only to grab a cup of tea. Cocooned in a puffy mound of warmth, she slept well and deeply.

Fírinne yawned and stretched, letting her body greet the day. Her cells drank in the salt air wafting off the chilly vistas open before her. She felt cold, a trace of fathomless chill in the air her senses could not quite place. The cold of deep space? The feeling made no sense as it moved through her waking body. "Time," her inner impulse whispered. "It is time."

The teacup she had brought to bed gleamed slightly in the dim pre-dawn light. The woodland scene etched onto the white porcelain made her smile. An image of the Earth Mother as Crone, flowing white tresses spread over a landscape in the embrace of its winter sleep, seemed to smile back at her. I love you," she whispered to the Great Mother. Then, suddenly, she was absorbed in vision.

Fírinne saw the deeply lined face of another ancient crone. The woman was quietly absorbed in tending a cauldron hung above a wood fire. Behind her was a white winter landscape. Falling snow hushed any hint of breeze. Even the crackle and hiss of the fire were dampened. The only discernible movement was the arm of the woman, quietly stirring. She was so ancient, and yet somehow familiar.

"The Cailleach!" Fírinne's mind supplied. "Bringer of storms and winter. She who is Brighid's counterpart. Is that true? What are you here to show me?"

With that thought, the fire in her vision flared, red-orange against the milky orb of a full moon. It turned the falling snow pink, drawing Fírinne's attention deeper.

"Something is coming," thought Fírinne as she allowed the vision to take her. "Why are you here?" she whispered to the Crone.

"Why are you here?" said the Crone's voice, though her lips did not move. "What do you remember about the snow moon?"

Fírinne's memory stirred in time with the Earth Mother's ladle. She looked, and she remembered. Stirring, stirring, the cauldron of life, the Crone's abundant hair was white with wisdom. It moved softly, waving with each circle of her shoulder.

Fire from ice.
Earth's awakening.
From the depths of the deepest cold,
is born the warmth of Spring.

Imbolc! These words were an invocation for Imbolc, a tribute to the Celtic Goddess, Brighid. This day holds a turning! Imbolc, traditionally celebrated on the 1stof February, celebrates the first signs of Spring and new beginnings. This is when seeds start to sprout, the first flowers bloom, and birds begin to sing again. It's as if the entire earth is waking up energized from its Winter slumber, ready to seize the new year.

With that quickening, snowdrops entered the vision, their tiny white trumpets bowed in gratitude and reverence for a new awakening from winter's sleep. Their sweet fragrance filled the frigid air, mingling with the fire's warmth, enticing fox, woodchuck, and bear to emerge, however fleetingly, from their dens into the light. Guardians of stealth, home, and courage took their places in the firelight. The forest was awake and waiting. Fire and moonlight mingled, birthing a new beginning.

Fírinne shivered as the palpable silence of the wild filled her field. Oh, how she loved the thrumming silence of the wilderness. But where was this, and what was she here to learn?

Her heart swelled as her vision deepened. "What is true about this?" had been her favorite question long before she learned to speak. "Tell me the truth!" she had demanded of her parents. Later, as she grew, she asked Source, "Show me the truth, no matter what." Now, she wondered, "Where is the truth beyond the image? Why does this vision matter now?"

Vision released her long enough for a bio break. With the deep forest filling her field, she stretched her legs. Padding to the cabin's tiny kitchen in thick woolen socks, Fírinne put the kettle on. The feeling of hardwood flooring confused her senses, still filled with the underfoot crunch of snow.

The forest of her vision began to fade as her eyes looked out at a grey winter's sea. Snow had fallen overnight. The bluffs around her lay clothed in soft, white powder, mirroring the stars' fading light. "Ah," she whispered, "not so different after all."

The kettle's whistle called her away from the window. It was a steaming reminder of practical things. Rubbing her arms against the cabin's chill, she put another log on the fire, then pulled her favorite jumper over her head. She loved the smell of this jumper, "sweater," as some call it. It smelled faintly of lanolin from the wool of black sheep, a fond memory of home. The fire crackled as the new log caught, and Fírinne grinned as she topped off the jumper with a handy shawl. "Home," she sighed. "Where will that be?"

"This is close," she whispered to the stars and the coming dawn. "This will do, for now." Cozily swaddled, grounded at this nexus of earth, sky, and sea, she stilled her mind.

Turning to the kettle, she poured steaming comfort into her cup. The image on its side brought her back to her earlier vision. The Great Mother as Earth Crone, her hair spread across the land, her smile lit forest, stone, and sea. Letting her nose delight in the caressing steam from her tea, Fírinne curled into one corner of the loveseat facing the sea.

She closed her eyes, then opened them. Surrounded by a white world framed by a silver sea, she allowed her mind to remain still. So, she had been trained for many years, and so she waited. Still the mind, let all the worlds go. Let wisdom unfold from the heart. Those instructions lived within her now.

Her inner eye caught sight of an approaching orb of light. Glowing within the whiteout of the landscape around her was a geometric shape, an icosahedron of transparent sapphire light. The image settled, front and center in her vision as if to announce its presence. Its blue luminescence shone around and through everything around her.

A stray thought entered her mind. "Why not a smooth orb for the full moon?" She noticed the idea without entertaining it. The orb began to glow with an inner light, almost as though her thought had been heard. As she stayed with the image, she felt the orb's emanation move into Gaia's energetic field like the bud of a rare flower. Then, unfolding one facet at a time, the infusion of incandescent blue merged into the energy field of pearlescence introduced with the last full moon. Its presence was exquisitely delicate yet radiated steely strength. Filaments and fibers of sapphire luminescence threaded through the room, the snow, and the world.

If she focused on the feeling of the pearly pink-white light from the last lunation, she could feel the Hathors' presence. If she focused on what was incoming, she felt the forest, the sea, and all living forms of the world. The images were distinct yet not separate. This is Mother magic, whispered through her heart.

Fírinne blinked once or twice and took a sip of still-hot tea. The vision had taken her out of time. What had seemed to take hours had taken only a few moments. "It happens today," she reminded herself again. "This full moon window is the next step in a re-creation of reality. Its exact alignment is today. Moonlight is a reflection of starlight. What celestial energies are involved?"

She looked for the star Sirius in the pre-dawn sky. She felt its presence, though she could not see it. Nevertheless, she felt the deepest of the sapphire light streams emanating through that system. Then she noticed a flash from Arcturus. Of course. She would have recognized this blue-white light anywhere. "Gaia must be receiving infusions from both systems," her mind offered.

Always the mind, a low voice chuckled. *Listen with your heart.*

Shushing her thoughts, Fírinne continued her inner observation. She noticed bits of structure carried within the infusion of blue-white light. Her mind translated familiar shapes into construction materials. Templates like girders, joins, and stabilizers streamed into Gaia's electromagnetic field. And then she heard the voice of Source within the transmission.

These elements will be needed. Collaborating with a new, fluid foundation, these elements will create new worlds.

The download of the vision that followed absorbed Fírinne's awareness entirely. She could not have moved had she tried. Instead, her fingers felt the heat dissipating from her mug of tea as timelessness took over.

Feel the infusion of Sapphire.

The beloved, unmistakable voice of Source was felt rather than heard. It resonated within every cell of Fírinne's body, each a galaxy in its own right.

Strands of Sapphire essence are the gift of the second jewel of thirteen. Sapphire is a wisdom vibration. Each of its hues represents a unique strand of stellar knowing. With delicate yet powerful energy, these light lines are coming in to replace much of what was. Many recall a blue-white light of Galactic Creation through whose portals they incarnated. Higher octaves of this light are now streaming into Gaia's realms to purify and fortify the basis of new reality constructs.

From a frozen, blind cycle comes new hope and possibilities. So much is shifting, though the many outcomes of these shifts are only beginning to manifest physically.

What has been repressed and hidden will be thrust into the light. This infusion is a force of renewal and transformation, rising through the depths of consciousness as though from the sea bottom.

"Life begins in the sea," Fírinne mused as the vision continued. "Was that from biology class?" She wondered what was true while her sight swam with pre-Cambrian era images. "What was this world like before there was atmosphere enough to breathe? What would Gaia become?"

As Fírinne wondered, her mind began to unpack the energies received. She shook her head, like a dog shedding water, willing her heart to take over. From that perspective, she felt Source's love cradling the celestial infusion of light. She felt the Cailleach, secreted in the deep woods, stirring the cauldron of life. Soothing and comforting her body and mind, Source's voice spoke of awakening, welling up from within.

The full snow moon is one of awakening. Feel the deep currents as they begin to move. Something is stirring beneath Gaia's crust and within you, too. A transition begins from inward gestating energy, to outward sprouting energy, and stirring releases steam. Each bud carries its blossom.

What within you is preparing to bloom?

Slowness is key. There is peace and stillness to the snow moon. Action is coming, but it is yet to be. Life is moving, but the effects are yet to be seen. Pay attention to what lies beneath.

Logs crashed in the fireplace, sending sparks and ash up the chimney. The fire was asking to be fed.

With that, Fírinne opened her eyes to the sunrise. The first rays of dawn danced over the snow, turning its crystals into prisms. Then, sparkles slid across the landscape, the morning breeze streaming crystals into the air and over the water. There, light met light in a spectacular display of gold-white-and-sapphire ripples, reflections, and rolling waves.

The deepest currents rolled into Gaia's energetic field with rich tones of sapphire. Fírinne remembered that the Sapphire stone is said to ease mental tension, bring peace and tranquility, and restore balance and harmony to the biofield or aura. It helps to align the spiritual plane with the physical. It is part of every sovereign and mystical tradition in the world. "Would this vibration change as well?" she wondered.

Lighter shades of blue and gold layered over the deep Sapphire energies within the incoming cosmic pulse. Each hue moved into a different realm of manifestation. Every atom, every particle of life, was bathed in and absorbed by this wave.

Fírinne gasped as the panorama took her breath away. She felt lost, absorbed in quantum waves of wonder. Her earlier vision of the winter forest reasserted itself, bringing a glimpse of integration. It began with nature, of course. She looked to the trees, wondering, and saw white-gold-blue light rods, like those she had seen in art exhibits, merging in spectral arrays within trunk, branch, and twig. The rods seemed a bit rigid, but upon closer observation, Fírinne recognized the structural forms of what was yet to be.

As she understood the seeding taking place, what had seemed to be light rods began to blend and swirl like the sky in Vincent van Gogh's painting, "Starry Night." The swirls of light took on the deep palette of the North Atlantic, moving into the turquoise spectrum of the South Pacific.

The light and the water. The water and the light.
The light is the water. The waters are the light.

"Yes," she thought, as cosmic love filled her heart in fractals of the flower of life. "Flow is love enacted through the elementals."

She grasped the tiny sound byte within her as treasure retrieved from long ago and far away.The elementals are the first to absorb new frequencies. Yet, she knew this understanding was only a beginning and an ending of all she had known.

Fírinne rose, tossed another log onto the fire, placed the grate in front of its glowing embers, and made a fresh cup of tea. As she resumed her seat near the windows, she reached out, tracing ice crystals at the base of the glass with the tip of one finger. Sunlight appeared behind the layer of ice as if summoned. The crystals glowed, blinding her outer vision. Fiercely gentle, the download intensified.

"Be present and surrender," the wind and the sea roared their herald to Source's transmission.

The full snow moon is an invitation to surrender. Let go of all needs and all impulses to control. Remember, I AM the doer and determine every outcome for the best as you allow me to weave your way. Trusting this, you enter into the dance of co-creation. Trust in divine timing; what is meant for you will be yours. Let go.

Remember that transformation and growth need not be loud. Radical change can be quiet, even silent, and still move mountains.

With that, the transmission ceased. Fírinne's physical sight cleared, and she stretched her body through what appeared to be finely wrought planes of crystalline light. She stood to regain feeling in her legs and bowed her thanks to earth, sky, and sea.

She shuffled a bit unsteadily into the bedroom. Then, placing her teacup carefully on the bedside table, she lay down to let the vision integrate. "What a wonder! What gifts these jewels bring." Snowdrops, growing wild beneath the inland-facing window, sang gently. Their sweet crystalline tones resonated with the surrounding snow, assisting her body in relaxing. "Thank you," she breathed to their delicate blossoms. "Thank you for your support."

As she surrendered utterly, she began to spin. Was it the room, the world, or the cells of her body? Fírinne couldn't tell. She didn't care. What did it matter?

Deeper. Go deeper, still.

This time, Source's voice resounded like a deep sonar ping, plumbing the depths beneath the waves of download and entering Gaia's core. Responding currents harmonized with the deepening sound.

"We are here. We are awake. It is time." Dragons! The stellar heart of Gaia thrummed and fluttered, pulsing with higher octaves of love, light, and frequency. Fírinne felt her own heart do the same until, finally, her body succumbed to sleep.

She must have slept the morning away. Bright sunlight lay across her pillow, making her shade her eyes as she swung her legs over the edge of the bed. Blinking, still a bit unsteady, she realized her teacup was empty, and the fire in the other room had gone out. Returning to the kitchen, she realized she had yet to eat. "In a minute," she thought as she gazed out at the sun on the sea. Filling the kettle and putting it on to boil once more, she headed for the door.

Donning boots, mitts, and parka, she ventured into the sun, whose barely felt warmth turned the world into crystals. With thundering booms, wind and waves rose to greet her. The wind whipped her hood, its icy breath rippling against her cheeks. She felt alone in all this magical world until the tiniest of movements caught her eye.

A shy fox stopped its stealthy jaunt along the low stone wall that marked the garden's edge and looked Fírinne in the eyes. These eyes glowed golden. The fox's body was all awash in incandescent light swirls like those of the transmission. "My body looks like yours," they felt together. The fox's bark echoed Fírinne's laughter. What a glorious day. What a magnificent passage this was to be.

The kettle's whistle called Fírinne indoors. Time for tea. Time for sustenance. "Time for me," she thought to the growing light. "I wonder who that will be?"

March

Cosmic Currents of the Eagle Moon

It took a bit of inner juggling for Fírinne to transition from one jewel to the next. Still held within the Pearl-supported Sapphire infusion, she felt only hints as to where she ought to be to experience the full moon of March. She felt aspects of depth and altitude; somehow, these elements needed to come together. It was not a simple case of "as above, so below." This was a simultaneous infusion, multidimensional in its intensity. Was there a perfect location, or was she trying to push the river?

A memory spoke to her. She remembered sitting on a beach on Kauai in the Hawaiian Islands. One life was dying, and another was beginning. It had been a karmic completion for so many things in her life. Relationship, home, career, everything she had counted on for so many years was gone. She remembered thinking, "I'm dying to be me," and laughed at Source's sense of humor. She remembered sitting in meditation on that beach, feeling like she was sitting on a mountaintop surrounded by sea instead of air. A new life was beginning, and Gaia supported it unconditionally.

Of course, these islands were volcanically created and rose above the water eruption after eruption. What an odd feeling it was to experience altitude at sea level. Had that been a preview of the next immersion experience? The memory had arrived for a reason, but Fírinne could not sense what that was. She had felt awash in cosmic seas while sitting up and above everything in this world. Exquisite! That was it. That was the feeling she had to find.

Fírinne had almost decided to stay where she was and experience the next transmission in meditation when a place she had always loved spoke to her. "I will always be shown," she sighed with relief. Gathering her hiking gear, she drove from one mountain range to another, feeling the energy lines rippling and racing beneath her as she went.

A few hours later, after stopping for the few provisions she might need, Fírinne headed to the hidden car park at the base of a favorite trail. With all the sand and loose rock, the canyon could not be negotiated without an all-wheel drive.

Twenty minutes uphill from the hidden turnoff and a short straight climb up a cliff yielded its reward. Wing shadows crossed her path, painting curious patterns on the mountainside. She had yet to climb this high without encountering eagles. Their play seemed to welcome her, as did the stone she sat upon. Not yet swollen with meltwater, the creek gurgled and rushed far below, adding its voice to the quiet symphony of height and beauty. If she tilted her head just so, Fírinne could smell the liquid freshness flowing down the mountain from its source at the lake, several thousand feet above. Pine, Juniper, and the burgeoning buds of Aspen greeted her gaze. Not quite spring, she mused, taking in the snow-capped peaks at her back, but a new light was dawning.

Fírinne returned to this location led by impulses of height and vastness. Though she had lived nearby for several years, the grandeur of this place never failed to move her. She hoped the dragon seat, as she called it, would be secure enough for her to embody the next infusion, the next jewel of Thirteen.

Mountains have deep roots. Fírinne could feel them beneath her and smell them in the new growth on the grandmother Sequoias and the forest of Juniper spread out across the foothills. She sat on a favorite perch, her dragon seat, formed of two quartzite slabs resting at 90 degrees to one another, atop a three-story high quartzite formation whose presence in that particular cliffside made no geological sense.

The slabs of rock formed a perfect chair. Afternoon sun warmed the cold stone, but still, she was glad of the rug she had brought to sit on. She could feel the humming of the quartzite beneath and around her as the ever-present breeze caressed her face. As she settled in, she wondered about altitude and air movement. 'The peaks affect the currents, and the winds shape the peaks,' her inner voice responded. Of course. Nature has her dance and her unique choreography. "Do the ethers move around us or through us," she wondered? "Yes," came the answer from every elemental at play.

Settling into her perch and sending a greeting to the pair of eagles riding the thermals above, Fírinne removed her boots and wedged them safely into a crevice protected from the wind.

Sitting cross-legged in her sturdy socks and jumper, she turned her face to the sun, inhaling deeply as the comforting scents of warm wool and altitude soil wafted their perfume on the breeze. Her four-legged companions had told her that quartzite smells different than granite, and today, she had to agree. Today, each scent held a singular vibration.

Worm moon, eagle moon. Heights. Altitude. Mountains. Fírinne felt prepared. The height, the chill, and the depths of rootedness filled her awareness. The wave she had been feeling for days toppled the tower of her inner identity as the transmission began.

It was specific, this tower. It represented an edifice of egoic identity, something she believed about herself that projected outward into the world. With the Virgo moon, the identity was likely to be the sovereign priestess and her shadowlands of unworthiness, undeservedness, and self-doubt. "I thought I was done with that," Fírinne muttered, knowing that the deep purging of this passage was bringing up every dormant seed and remnant of other lives lived within this one.

The truth of the sovereign priestess was her alignment with the patterning of cycles, rhythms, and the natural timings within and without.

A tower of false belief was coming down, replaced by a more profound understanding. Shame had been welling up for days, burning through her awareness in memory after memory of things Fírinne was not proud of having done or said. She knew a bardo experience when she felt one and had offered each memory, each flash of heat, anger, fear, and shame, to the Source within. She knew that inner change always happens first. Energy always occurs first. Vibration always happens first. These truths would be critical in navigating this year's passage. And, still, the burning had stung.

Feel the changes. Look with your inner eyes. Listen with your Hathor ears.

Source's guidance filled Fírinne's heart with lightness. The part about Hathor ears made her giggle as she imagined her reflection with the large protruding ears of the statues she had seen in Egypt.

The orb of the next jewel had entered her awareness days ago. This one had not positioned itself in front of her inner sight but had moved cleanly and precisely into the starlit pulse of Gaia's crystalline center. From there, delicate lines of light began to shape things around the planet. Each new strand moved into the electromagnetic lines of the world, amplifying their highest octaves of frequency and allowing new energies to enter. "Widening the road," Fírinne thought with a grin.

The Aquamarine orb pulsing through bud, branch, and stone sharply contrasted the greens and browns of high desert, alpine forest, and the cerulean blue sky. This orb, softer in form than the first two, glowed with a cool integrated fire. Was this what it offered? Fírinne could feel but not yet see. Her inner knowing indicated that these feelings were an initial transmission of essence. Any information would arrive with the coming Equinox and beyond.

Effortlessly permeating everything, a gentle Aquamarine flow flooded her awareness. As seawater carries the building blocks of all life, this pulse infused wave after wave of elemental energies through her heart, her third eye, and every cell of her body. Though she sat on stone, she felt that she was floating.

Allowing her awareness to sink into deep grounding within the stellar heart of Gaia, Fírinne noted that this swelling pulse had already filled Gaia's center and was re-arranging the planet's geometric structure from her core. Thread by infinite thread, lines of light formed, and realities were re-woven. The pristine clarity of creation was breathtaking.

She watched a simultaneous crystalline growth extend outward from the Earth's core and waves of pulsing gentleness flowing into infinity. She could feel the inner workings of this, coming through the roots of the mountain, the worm moon bringing the massive strength of earthworms digesting and moving the soil far below.

Earthworms move mountains by creating underground ripples like the wind makes waves in the sea. As Fírinne felt this, an eagle soared overhead. Eagles represent the ability to fly high and see the big picture, she remembered, with what was left of conscious thought. This was also an Eagle moon, bringing expanded vision, as the reflection of light closest to the Equinox. "And we are in that window," Fírinne breathed into the Oneness as it absorbed her completely.

Part of her decision to experience the infusion of the third jewel at the dragon seat was its altitude, clarity, and proximity to sacred vision. She had wondered how safe she would be sitting on this exposed ledge. What if her vision swept her away? Would she remember to be still and not endanger her physical body?

You are always taken care of, echoed within. She remembered those words well and relaxed into the care of the Sacred Unseen.

As perspectives of depth and height merged, Fírinne's vision expanded. The coming integration felt like a fluid envelope, containing the birth waters for the welling up of what was to come. Structured water, she remembered. We are structured water. And what of the jewel?

Fírinne considered the qualities of the stone Aquamarine. She felt its clear, calm toning through the Earth's magma. She remembered that it is said to calm, cleanse, and purify. An excellent ally in meditation, if put into water, it is said to cleanse those waters and make them into a healing pool, pond, bath, or river, wherever one has placed the stone.

The voice of Source flowed gently through her mind, interrupting her train of thought.

Infused into the waters of life, these frequencies of gentle cleansing and building of strength assist the transition.

As she imagined an orb of Aquamarine, attempting to sense its exact purpose, its energies pulsed immediately, dissolving into a resonating, spherical morphing wave. On and on, this wave expanded from Gaia's center, beyond the horizon, the solar system, and out toward the edge of the galaxy, taking Fírinne's awareness with it. "This is so much larger than we know," she breathed to the rocks that supported her. "Everything is changing. Will we recognize anything after its passing?

"This wave is cresting, and it won't come back down. Instead, it's going to turn into seas on the move. So here we have what's moving underneath and then this soaring view of what is possible, of how things might be. This wave is truly a fresh start."

Fírinne knew she was watching the power of vibration in the process of transformation, creating and holding form, wholeness, and manifestation. The contents of the pulsing waves were so immense that she had no recourse but to let go and be carried within them, letting her Observer lie dormant for a time.

This wave is the budding of nature in the Northern Hemisphere and the budding within all selves. This jewel is coming through the perspective of the Eagle, of seeing above everything that has happened while feeling those worm giants in the underworld, in the topsoil, that are moving mountains of energy beneath your feet. This is a ramp-up to the new frequency platform that the coming Equinox represents.

Clinging to her Observer function, Fírinne realized she had packed a small journal in her gear sack. She opened her eyes, intending to rummage for it, and nearly lost her seat. The meditation had felt like sea level. Her body took a minute to recalibrate how high she was and to balance within the waves at this altitude.

She began to write, letting nature guide her pen. The implement felt odd in her hand until she released herself into nature's flow. Her fingers trembled with the massive current of truth. "If there is ONE TRUTH, how is that moving through this?" Her long-cherished internal quest exploded into light as her fingers tried to obey the command to write.

Source's beloved voice resonated through Fírinne's body.

It is not what you ARE, but what you believe yourselves to be that perishes. You are moving through a great morphing of the heart.

At that moment, she realized that this jewel, this liquid flow of Aquamarine frequency, carried an elemental influx that would feed the strata of higher frequencies arriving with each alignment until and through the Solstice in December. It was almost too much for her mind to take in.

This is an energetic influx of what needs to be. This is a new perspective of the heart.

Fírinne closed her eyes again, wanting to feel and embody what was being offered as deeply as possible. She felt the spherical morphing wave moving through her heart, third eye, energy centers, and every cell in her body. These pulses were synchronized yet individuated to their purpose. What had begun with the sonar ping of Sapphire infusion expanded into the varied and vibrant hues of tropical seas. No wonder Aquamarine had shown up as an ally! The notion of 'touchstone' echoed among cosmic currents of laughter.

At that moment, all inner motion ceased. Everything came to a still point. From this silence arose joy, rapture, and a rebalancing into more organic timings within whose currents the old ways would not stand. Fírinne watched the old world break up and dissolve. Tower after tower, fell. Neil Young's lyrics played through her heart, "It's only castles burning..." There was no fire, but only dissolution.

When she opened her eyes, she saw ripples of clear light moving through peaks and valleys, trees and clouds, as though everything had turned to liquid, made of the flowing plasma of essential being. The cells of her legs flowed, along with the rock they sat folded upon.

Coming slowly back into her body, she realized she was chilly. Attending the practical first, she put on her boots and jacket, remembering a more manageable way down the mountainside, a path off to her right. It would take her a bit farther from her car, but would be a good idea in her altered state. Dangling her newly booted feet from the ledge, she took deep centering breaths. The quartzite tower no longer reflected the sun's heat. It was almost sunset. It was time to leave.

Climbing carefully out of the dragon seat, Fírinne thanked everything she could think of for the privilege of witnessing this event. She had enjoyed many mystical experiences in her life, yet Source's invitation to take an active part in this passage still blew her away. She hoped the wind would not attempt the same, as she began her trek down the mountain.

The mountainside held her feet as she made her way along. She felt a gentle acknowledgment that she and the Earth had played this game for ages. Whenever she asked, the stone and standing people always answered with unerring support.

"Hungry!" her body told her. She hadn't eaten much for the past three days. She took a long drink from her water bottle and promised to feed herself soon. Among the provisions she had purchased earlier were an apple and a bag of almonds. That would have to do for now.

Wondering what the Equinox waves would bring, and dreaming of grilled cheese, she pulled out of her secluded parking spot and turned toward town. Fields and forests rippled with an upwelling of liquid crystalline flow. She pulled over, twice, only to realize that her field was rippling as well.

"I wonder if this is what a caterpillar feels as it liquifies?" she thought as she settled herself behind the wheel and pulled out onto the main road.

April

The Salmon Moon ~ Jade

Salmon are the wise, sacred fish of the Celts, associated with the Aois Dana, the Poets of Ireland. Large, powerful, and embodying the fertile golden glow of the Sun in their flesh, inspirational in their courage and knowledge, the salmon are honored as sacred symbols of wisdom. That wisdom includes an unerring ability to return upriver from the sea, completing their species' cycle of rebirth.

During this moon tide, Fírinne would be a mental traveler. She knew by how altered she felt in the aftermath of the Equinox. An energetic plateau arrived with that alignment, raising all that could now thrive in higher frequencies directly into those realms. She could hardly look at anything in nature without seeing its plasmic ripples. It was not a time to drive anywhere if the immersion was to be entirely honored!

The full moon of April would be an inner infusion. She could already feel it in her heart. Where would the inner journey begin? There is always a location of inception, a vortex of receptivity that calls out to any infusion. Images of budding trees and salmon lunging upstream to complete their life cycles filled Fírinne's mind. So did the brilliant green glow spreading throughout her body. The next jewel had already arrived. Its bright green orb pulsed gently through her energetic field.

Her first impression was that Anahata, the heart chakra, tends to glow green, but that thought was immediately swept aside as though by a lion or dragon's paw. Source's voice echoed through her head,

That is what your mind thinks it knows. Look and listen.

And with the directive to listen came the memory of standing on the South Island of New Zealand, feeling the voices of the stones. The winds spoke, the seas spoke, and the tides contributed their harmonies. Fírinne felt an inner knowing that this particular orb brought back ancient tides filled with new stellar connections. "The stars have ever guided us," she thought, as her mind wondered, "which stars?" Maybe if she could recognize a constellation overhead, she would know where to listen.

Was there a location of focus to guide her vision? Source's voice whispered,

Aotearoa. New Zealand. Remember how you felt standing at the nexus of land, sky, and sea. Remember the songs of that vortex.

How could she forget? The experience had left an indelible imprint. Whenever she tuned in to the memory, whale song followed. Within it flowed the essence of the luminous "Goddess of Peace." Fírinne knew her only as the White Goddess, glowing with divine light, She of many names from many cultures. The nurturing Presence Fírinne had denied during her long years of patriarchal spiritual training flowed through this land 'down under.' "Of course," she murmured. "Nurturing energy. The Goddess of Peace."

The jewel of transformation for this moon moved vivid green light through her body. It sang of reconnection, new stargates, and a re-calling of the understanding that when we hold a stone in hand, we hold the stars.

She sat outdoors, in the garden, beneath friendly trees. She had become increasingly absorbed, all day, into frequencies that shone like the Emerald City of Oz. Rather than a tide washing over her, these welled up from the Earth's core and her own.

Fírinne felt the ground beneath her, the entwined roots of the Aspens that towered above her head and cast their seeds wide, ever attempting to expand their sacred groves. This past Autumn, the cascading gold of their canopy created a tremulous, transiting temple of golden glow. With spring buds now about to burst, their tender branches sang to her as they danced in the slightest breeze.

High altitude sun is intense, no matter the season, so she adjusted her position to rest beneath the Aspens' rooted and stretching strength. "Help me to ground," she whispered, laying her head back against the smooth whiteness of the closest trunk.

With that thought, her awareness shifted. She felt lifted from her mountain garden, over and across the seas.

She could feel sand beneath her bare feet and sea grass underneath her body as she lay near the shore. Salt air caressed her nose and cheeks as she surrendered to the sound of the ebb and flow of the waves. A subtle presence surrounded and carried her.

Fírinne had experienced this presence through many Goddess archetypes, most recently the archetypal field of White Tara, Mother of all Buddhas. But this Divine embrace permeated the land in New Zealand. It rang through the ever-present whale song, filling every fiber of her being with reverence and gratitude. "Thank you," she breathed, knowing she had her starting point.

"Show me," Fírinne whispered to the Presence, the moon's reflected light and the flow of wholesome greening. For days, a glowing sphere of green swelled within her chest. She had been unsure which stone would present itself as the next jewel. Its essence had to be heart-related. She knew that much. And, she was aware that most of the world's green stones had at least a thread of heart essence, one way or another.

Some stones are receptive to love in an extraordinary way.

"Jade," mused Fírinne. "And not just any Jade, but the Pounamu of Aotearoa."

The stone, Pounamu, begins its journey in the seas, moving from beneath the sea floor as magma, rising into the heights of the Southern Alps through long ages of time. From these heights, it then falls, shaken by seismic tremors and ferocious storms, to crumble into avalanches of sacred grounding. It journeys downhill, finding home in lakes and rivers, until it reaches the sea, sinking into welcoming sands to begin its ages-long journey once again. Those who remember and carry this wisdom collect the Pounamu stones only with the stone's permission and that of the land from which it comes.

"I don't own any Pounamu," she thought, as if any stone could be owned. "Its sacredness is a gift the land has not chosen to give me. So perhaps this will do for now." Then, sitting in the garden behind the house, turning a bracelet of Chinese Jade around her left wrist, she asked the stone for its song and stilled her mind to listen.

The Jade orb vibrated. "My essence moves physically from the infinite unto eternity. I represent the journey from the alone to the alone, written in the Vedas. I am the mineral equivalent of the Great Mother's love."

She remembered reading that Jade holds a luminous earth element energy. It is traditionally known to connect heaven and Earth, creating an alignment of balance. Jade also symbolizes gentleness, serenity, harmony, and the particular essence of calming that alleviates fears. It is a stone of strength, luck, and great abundance.

What she had read merged with the green gold around her as the stone circling her wrist and that of far-off Pounamu began to sing.

Dense green honeylike energy flowed through her body into light rods like those she had seen with the Sapphire infusion. These rods moved within her bone marrow, through her skull, into grey matter, and beyond. They seemed to solidify into a tubular form, then dissolve entirely. On closer observation, she felt her cellular makeup shifting. The purity of green essence modified her cellular structures from the nucleus outward through every particle in her body's elementals. How would she be changed? Her body seemed to understand what her mind could not.

This was unlike the last psychic infusions. Those energies formed new timelines and trajectories that would make their way into physical manifestation following global shifts in frequency. This was matter radiating cleanly and purely, shifting itself beyond any semblance of human interference.

Fírinne saw this tide as the beginning of the completion of the gestation of something long-remembered, perhaps thought lost, and altogether new. Words failed as the tide enfolded her awareness. Through the land, the stones, and the seas, the cells of her body flooded with honoring, nurturing, and reverence for all of life.

Voices of whales lifted her Spirit as she closed her eyes and moved deeper into vision. While on the islands, her greatest joy had been the constant immersion in whale song. It became so much a part of her that she only noticed its absence. Of course, that had been in a shopping mall car park, with too many humans and silly wants clogging up the airwaves.

Otherwise, she had felt continually afloat in the grace of the song of these magnificent creatures. Their voices lulled her into restful silence within the embrace of the land.

Fírinne surrendered more deeply to the essence of harmony, balance, and peace, emanating through her body as the song of the stone supplied reams of information. Source spoke to her, that treasured voice mingling with the song.

The essence of Jade can be a touchstone for how best to navigate a turbulent time.

Fírinne began to receive images of Egyptian temples and the Goddess Ma'at. The Goddess held her heart in the balance, aligned with every imagined concept of peace. "When a heart is weighed against a feather, is there lightness enough to create harmony within that light?" Fírinne felt her heart, both heavy and light, balancing in unimagined ways. These ways moved entirely outside the domains of ego or personality, taking hold ever more firmly in her physical body. She felt the deep, healing green filling each cell. Every breath drew it deeper in.

She felt a heaviness in the bones of her face and jaw, a tension that spread down her right side into her toes. She knew it was shadow and remained focused on the green glow permeating her blood vessels, meridians, and muscle tissue.

This glow is the wholeness that replaces old hurt.

The song of the stone soothed her body as she continued to listen. She knew the Libra moon alignment, exact at 16 degrees, 7 minutes, offered another Tower opportunity. What tower of identity was being demolished? When an egoic tower falls, our inner knowing, our trust in Source, must shift.

The tower being decimated by this wave of wholeness releases what is out of balance into the light. What new lightness will you begin to ground within? Not within yourself, but as yourself, within that lightness, as a drop in my Infinite sea?

Fírinne thrilled to Source's voice in those words and the sounds and songs surrounding her. Fully absorbed, she could only listen.

What has been obliterated by challenging situations or 'storms'? Even things built on solid foundations can be swept away by the tidal forces of transition or by emotional silt dredging up for release. Here, within the mystery of connection, do you feel safe? How do you feel unsafe? This is where your emotions are not grounded in my loving embrace. Let go and allow.

Where are your relationships between aspects of yourself lacking tenderness? The Libra Moon encourages sweetness, beauty, gentle comfort, and the peace of inner justice.

Within her vision, Fírinne felt the Jade bracelet slide on her arm. The physical sensation reminded her that though her body was in one location and her sight in another, there was unity in this transmission and in receiving it.

"This is the high trail," sang the whales, "The Trail of Spirit."

One of the traditions of Aotearoa is that of the Waitaha. These peoples followed the teachings of Rongomaraeroa, the way of Peace. Every particle of earth, sea, and sky was revered and honored as sovereign, intelligent, and of the collaboration of life. Pounamu is sacred to this sea-faring, life-honoring people as they journeyed far afield to protect a cohesive peace.

"I remember," she sang to the stone." I honor your presence and your love."

"What are we willing to honor within ourselves and one another?

What is the balanced harmony of the Sacred within us all? What is that worth?"

Fírinne watched in horror as a magnificent piece of Pounamu was dashed from its sacred bedding, tumbling far afield until it came to rest in a river bottom, unseen except by Source's eyes. "What can be done to rescue this bit of sacredness? Where has it landed?" Fírinne's heart ached to help.

This infusion is the next octave of grounded inner guidance. Then, like the salmon for which this moon is named, like the star-guided Pounamu, you can find your way home again. It may be the dikes and barriers constructed to control your inner flow that now need to be demolished.

The collective vibration of this planet is rising, causing the manifestation of the shadow that has been hiding inside.

All this and more poured through Fírinne's body, mind, and heart. The dense green honeylike energy flowed through her, glowing with health and healing. And, for the moment, her physical pain intensified.

"Everything begins with vibration and with sound," the whales sang. "This wave carries the song of wholeness, wellness, and harmonized physicality. The ancient tides are pregnant with new stellar connections. These are birthing tides, not yet released.

"This is a passage of physically trusting the Source Essence of all things," the song continued. "Within all tempestuous waters, there flows a stillness, a sanctuary, a current connected to the Oneness, and the specific points of light that move through our incarnated bodies like the stars.

"This is the high trail," sang the whales. "The Trail of Spirit."

And with that, Fírinne's body was released.

Fírinne moved a bit, surprised to be back in her garden and realizing her body had become stiff and sore. As she shifted, the gold-green glow rushed through blood vessels and meridians as if commanded. The support of the Rockies was palpable, the crisp scent of fresh snowfall on the peaks a sharp contrast to her experience of lying close to the sea.

She opened and closed her eyes several times, but the vision did not fade.

She saw salmon swimming upriver after the melt. She heard the melody of the meltwaters. Such a fascinating song! It spoke of freeing things that have been frozen, a feast of new waters, opportunities, recreating, and reconnecting with the circle of Oneness.

The reciprocity of caregiving and care-receiving flowed throughout the cosmos, the multiverse, playing through Fírinne's vision like a surging sea. She felt the truth of the harmony, the balance, and the peace that now nestled in her heart.

Like the salmon, she was completing a circle. Coming home, here, in this body and this place, wherever that was to be. She grasped onto the first coherent words her mind received.

Truth is the song of your essence.

Opening her eyes, Fírinne reached for her journal. Then, writing as fast as she could, she let words pour directly from Source onto the page.

It is time for ancient ways and new stellar information to harmonize and integrate within our bodies. As this lovely orb of incandescent green light integrates, it creates a new heart. Some will feel and know.

Others will not. Be patient with those in resistance. They do not understand what they are going through. Their bodies will let them know.

A very visceral infusion will push out physical imbalances of every kind. It is bringing the new gestation of whatever will birth into physicality. This will surge. It will well up through your bodies, through the blood, through the meridians, through the muscles. As you remember that the stars are in the stones and the stones are of the stars, you will recognize that so, also, the stars are in your bones.

You are ambulatory stellar emanations. You all come from the same Source. Your differences are like light on the water. So beautiful when purely and clearly expressed.

Fírinne realized she had curled into a fetal ball, her knees hugged into her chest, her journal beside her. She was the salmon swimming upstream. Such a long journey it had been. She had ventured so far from home.

Like the salmon, she knew what she must do. Wise salmon knows its place; its fractal in the circle of life. Swimming upstream, she realized, is only a phase in the longer journey. The reflected starlight of this full moon held completion. It was a resurrection in the Oneness. She was not only infusing Spirit into matter, but remembering, literally re-membering, that matter is Spirit and that all is Source.

With that realization, a green glow washed through all the world as Fírinne grabbed her pen once more.

These are the beginnings of the birthing tides, she wrote. We have been gestating. All different worlds, lineages, times, and places are coming into alignment.

The light-lines of this world are changing from those of Gaia's stellar relations through her celestial heart, and particularly from the emanations of the way of peace. The tribes of the Waitaha knew and know this. This comes from a deep, deep elemental ancestry that is of Gaia herself. She is the mother of our bodies and the womb of our physical connections to our stars.

Each body is a fractal. All embodiments are connected to a specific star, stars, or constellations. All are drops in infinite waters. The stone that comes from the glaciers, down through the rivers, and offers itself as a gift from the land has not lost that connection. It is this knowing being reborn within all of nature. It is to be carried forward in a new way.

Like waters delivering a stone from the heights on its way to the sea, this beautiful green color is moving through the bodies of Gaia's residents very viscerally. This flow sings of the truth, sings of infinite connection. The way of peace, the way of sacred collaboration, is guiding this.

All beings can walk this trail guided by their stars and the Source within. And, like the salmon, all instinctively know their path on this Earth. This is home. It is a replacement for obsolete vibrations.

Fírinne stood, using the support of the Aspen tree to keep her upright. Leaning against its strength, she continued to listen. The writing would have to wait. She let the green world and its root systems ground the flow through her heart as Source's voice continued.

Surrender into what is surging, letting its energies impulse you as it rises through the land you call New Zealand. It streams through the glaciers, down through the rivers, and throughout the surrounding seas, through the volcanic action that created this landmass, and on through the sea floor. It moves from mountain to mountain and tree to tree instantaneously, as one particle synchronizes with another.

The land of Aotearoa communicates with the underlayers of the Tibetan Plateau. It is sparking there. It is flashing in Ireland, the Outer Hebrides, and other islands. The divine tide is rising in places where there is less of a human imprint or a more respectful human imprint, and more of an honoring of the magic of love's peace and harmony.

This tide is melting structures of hurt within you and all of nature. It moves within the awakening mountains of this world. There is a particular resonance happening that has to do with a specific resurgence of the way of peace.

This is the beginning of the surge, the culmination, the completion of the gestation. It will be a complete reconfiguration of all bodies. What is most important is that you honor this new alignment.

Occasional protective ferocity is needed. But that rises through the heart. It is different than dominance and control. Those structures are being replaced. This is a calming, grounding energy.

Learn to be that grounding, to walk that grounded flow of Source in a physical body.

Let truth walk this passage.

There is always a path of light through any darkness, any pain. This is a grounded flow of inner guidance with practical applications, although you have yet to learn what. You don't need to. You will be shown. This is the trust you must carry.

Garden sounds replaced Source's transmission. Letting birdsong, the chittering of squirrels, and the gentle breeze return her to her body, Fírinne blinked and sat up. She realized her body had collapsed into the shade of the aspen tree. Her left arm rested against its trunk, supporting her head. The cat curled on top of her feet, her feline body pulsing with green-gold tides. She seemed to want the grounding as much as she assisted it.

Fírinne thanked the trees, the land, the peaks glowing in the distance, and most of all, the stone. "And you, sweet kitty," she whispered, disengaging her legs from their feline embrace.

Laughing a bit as she shook her body awake, she wondered, "What will the next jewel bring?"

"Perspective," whispered the wind through the trees.

May

An Infusion of Perception ~ Amethyst

The next infusion began stealthily, with threads of purple energy mingling with the Jade essence in her body. It looked like a fiber-optic display of fluid dynamics or a map of wind currents. Amethyst merged into Jade as a new gem ally, carrying clear awareness of known, unknown, and rarely visited places in consciousness.

Fírinne's dragon guide appeared through a glowing portal of swirling golden-purple light. She hadn't visited in quite some time. Fírinne felt the dragon's call to rise and to ride. "What is different about this full moon's energies?" Fírinne wondered. "What are the gifts of nourishment they seed?"

"Vision and perspective," the dragon replied as she tossed her onto her back with a powerful twist of her supple golden body. Heaving her mighty tail, the dragon took to the skies.

Transforming through the portal she seemed to carry with her, the dragon manifested over the Himalayas, then flowed at what Fírinne would have called warp speed, lighting up the energies of peak after peak until she reached the northernmost tip of the European Alps.

The Jade infusion had rippled through the Southern Alps of Aotearoa, gifting its sacred energies to river and stream. Finally, its energies rolled through the sea floor of the South Pacific and into Gaia's crystalline heart. There, at home in Gaia's Oneness, it had seemed to disappear.

Now, Fírinne soared above Northern Alps. Somehow, a connection she had earlier felt between the Tibetan plateau and Aotearoa now asserted itself through Europe's great mountain chain. She supposed that, from Gaia's center, energy could flow anywhere it chose.

The dragon's body rippled with laughter as it sped higher and higher. Like the dragon, Fírinne's vision swept and flowed among the peaks. It circled the Zugspitz, blew past the Matterhorn, wove through the Tirol, and soared toward Italy and the Dolomites. Suspended in the pure consciousness of high altitude, Fírinne felt her body surrender to a new configuration. Her breathing slowed, and her vision expanded. She could see all the world from this vantage point. Even the curvature of the Earth was visible from this perspective.

Finally, her consciousness began to settle in the area of Mont Blanc. Its luscious melding of old-world, close-to-nature culture and state-of-the-art technology had always called forth her adventurer's spirit and held a place in her heart. The area reminded her of something, she did not know what. Somehow this part of the world had always felt like a piece of home.

Her mouth watered as her taste buds remembered the unpacking of flavor from delicious alpine cheese and artisanal saucisson, made with loving care. The odor of alpine herbs and flowers filled her senses, their songs rising on a sun-warmed breeze. Her dragon guide stretched and purred its pleasure at her enjoyment of nature's offerings. "You are here, in a body," she growl-purred as she flew. "You need to enjoy what life offers."

"This passage is one of new nurturing," Fírinne remembered.

"This infusion is a nurturing of perception."

What do you see when higher octaves present themselves? Will you tune into new fractals within new currents? What does the Eagle or Phoenix see that the butterfly cannot? What is the perspective of the dragon and its rider? Purity of spirit nurtures purity of perception.

All this Fírinne heard, and more. Source's transmission unpacked faster than Fírinne's mind could process it.

"Let go. Let your body and mine absorb and integrate together." There was a deeper meaning to the dragon's words, that the woman on her back could not yet fathom.

"Is this what it means to learn to ride the wind?" Fírinne's mind still grasped her earthly perspective, even as she rode and began to vibrate higher.

What is the feeling of Shambhala?

Source's reminder was timely indeed. Fírinne had always thought Shamballa to be a perspective of higher collaborative harmony. Legends spoke of such a civilization high in the mountains. But, to her, it had always felt like something inside herself. This alignment was something toward which she strove.

She had dedicated her whole life to the purity of higher consciousness. This infusion was intense, and moving into embodiment faster than her mind could track it. What was the gift it represented?

"Perspective from the heights," the dragon answered.

How was this perspective meant to be grounded? Was it accomplished by rooting, like a tree? Or, did the earthworms, giant earth-movers in their under-soil realm, have a more valid perspective?

"My mind is in the way again," Fírinne told herself as the dragon banked sharply, weaving itself around another peak.

Fírinne had read that this full moon, penumbral eclipse, and Bealtaine alignment would be a critical pivot point for shifting identity, for the images people sell themselves, mainly about themselves. As those images shift, all other images also tend to alter.

"The cross-quarter's vertical alignment was opening a column of light that cast no shadows. It was offering a deep dive into the mysteries, into what had previously been hidden. The penumbral eclipse, revealing lacy, soft edges of the Earth's shadow on one side of the moon, then the other, was allowing personal perceptions to shift to more accurate reflections.

The Scorpio properties of the full moon and the eclipse involve being unmasked. An eclipse is a form of an occultation, meaning something is shadowed or hidden. Its light will unmask many things, including what is truly within our hearts and any lingering self-perceptions."

Fírinne took a deep breath and let the book stuff, and herself, go. The alignment's Amethyst wave entered through the sphere of her perception, altering it completely. As a result, she perceived each nuance of vision in new ways.

As Jade's essence had replaced all that felt out of place in her body, this Amethyst essence replaced ideas and judgments about what she felt was important and sacred. The experience felt simultaneously jarring and revelatory. From her current vantage point, Fírinne clearly saw the sacredness of all of life.

As she soared through the mountain passes, she wondered at the reflections below. She was a fractal of every mirror; each experience was hers to explore.

Outdoor enthusiasts, like tiny ants, streamed far below, hiking the 100-mile circuit around Mont Blanc. Their stream of constant motion brought her memories of similar practices in the Himalayas. There, pilgrims travel long distances to walk upon sacred ground. Likewise, the threads of light from this transmission moved through Europe, illuminating every pathway, every trail, every potential step.

"Is there a part of every hiker aware that they tread on the sacred body of the Earth?" Boots had always felt holy to Fírinne. Perhaps this was why.

Her heart beat with the clanging of ceremonial cow bells as she witnessed small herds escorted down from the high meadows, whose lush grasses and sweet flowers were transformed, within the cows' bodies, into milk and then, by their farmers, into cheese. "This is alchemy as well," she thought.

She watched this autumnal parade down from the high pasture, during which the cows, adorned with bells and flowers, were honored for the gifts they give. Here in the high county, the gifts of these beings had been honored as long as bovine and human had lived together. These annual events celebrate the sacredness of life and the blessings of Mother Earth. Tradition holds that these animals are a source of goodness, and their milk nourishes all creatures.

Cows are sacred in Eastern traditions as well, where the cow represents the flow of life-giving milk and the essence of the Great Mother. They are a grounded example of why this galaxy is called the Milky Way. "Perhaps some of that ancient knowledge found its way here, long ago."

A pinkish-white glow surrounded that thought. Fírinne smiled as she recalled the Hathors' initial assistance with these transmissions. It seemed they had not abandoned the project but continued to guide its shape and form.

In Fírinne's experience, some of the most intense infusions are also the most subtle. The alteration of her entire perceptual field made her see with new eyes, revealing what had been hidden and obscuring what was no longer relevant. Another veil, or veils, had been pulled back in an instant.

She remembered reading something about this level of intensity, potentially feeling like toothpaste squeezed from a tube all at once. If someone did not allow the pressure to move them forward, it would squash them like a bug. This infusion made sense of that description but felt different. She felt pulled and stretched, rather than pushed. She sensed she was being extracted from a cocoon or womb, not by forceps but by that old world falling away from her acceleration. It felt like the cocoon of her old life was sinking, and her true nature was slowly and methodically lifting her from the undertow.

As the dragon circled, so did Fírinne's thought processes. "Why had the Amethyst gem volunteered as an ally for this full moon?" Known as the pink moon, the full moon of May is said to reflect the light of opening and blossoming. Its essence was always that of a heart opening. "Why amplify perception now?"

This infusion is a blossoming of heightened perception.

Drawn ever more inward, Fírinne remembered more from her training. She recalled that Amethyst is revered for enhancing spiritual awareness. It opens intuition and amplifies psychic abilities. In addition, it has substantial healing and cleansing powers for amplifying clarity, universal perspective, and purity of heart. Amethyst is also known to assist in aligning with and deepening inner peace.

Fírinne loved Amethyst. For her, the Amethyst stone had always held a protective energy. She loved wearing it and had placed several loose stones about her home. She found a sizeable silver-wrapped Amethyst point during her years of study and had worn it on and off ever since. That is, until a completion of Atlantean karmas made the stone want to move on. Maybe it was Fírinne who had moved on. She had made a gift of that treasure to a friend. "Was it the right thing to do?"

Your choices have led you here. Choose to be free.

Fírinne realized that she had felt incomplete without her longtime Amethyst ally. She missed its presence and felt she had not given it a proper goodbye, or so she thought. Then, she realized it was not her gifting of the stone essence that bothered her. Instead, it was the lack of respect from the alleged friend, who only wanted what she felt she could profit from and could not get away fast enough afterward.

Surrounded by frenemies, Fírinne had jettisoned everything from that phase of life as quickly as she could. And, from her current height, she saw that this had happened repeatedly, as needed. Over and over, an obsolete fractal of her learning cycle had been replaced by something more aligned with her path in this life. It had all been perfect. It had been time to let go.

All this, her newly opened perception showed her. Finally, her awareness returned to the dragon that carried her. She seemed to have been patiently circling the Alps, playing aloft in the thermals and swirls of energy rising from their depths. Then, with the return of Fírinne's attention, the dragon moved on.

The dragon and her rider continued to surge through the mountains, exchanging vibrational nourishment with each location. As they honored each peak, they experienced its gifts, miraculous beingness, and support for those who lived upon it.

"Mountains rise up in support of life," Fírinne realized. "Magma pushes to the surface to bring clean elemental energies to light."

Circling the Matterhorn toward Zermatt, Fírinne flowed through memories of local goats clanging through town every morning and evening. The town center was maintained as a clean energy area. No combustion engines were allowed. It seemed that was still the case, though it was hard to tell from this height.

Her dragon companion coasted alongside the cable cars and lifts that rise toward Monte Rosa, the highest peak in Switzerland. This area was surrounded by some of the world's finest engineered cogwheel trains, lifts, and funiculars, providing all comers the gift of height and vision, whether these gifts are fully understood or not.

Fírinne chuckled, "They ride the manufactured magic, and I get to fly!"

The Alps filled the horizon with jagged glory. Fírinne's attention was drawn earthward from the breathtaking spectacle to the glowing undulation of the Glacier Express train, winding through peaks and valleys. She knew the train traveled from Zermatt to Saint Moritz. She couldn't think why that mattered until the train's tall windows gleamed in the sunlight, reminding her of the scales of the dragon she rode. "Are there dragon ley lines beneath these peaks? Will they flow here more strongly now that the world was changing?"

Her flight followed the course of the rivers that flowed through valleys shaped by glaciers, supplying the area with fresh water. "Water," thought Fírinne. "Another gift of nurturing." What other gifts would show themselves to her regenerated perceptual field?

The town of Appenzell, one of the key locations at the heart of Swiss independence, appeared beneath her. This town was originally formed from the union of a few cantons against the Hapsburg empire, splitting the various alliances in the region. She felt the mirror of competing world factions. It made her sad, and asked for more clarity.

"Independence," growled the dragon.

"Of course. Independence and its embodiment of freedom. More gifts some humans tend to fight for or take for granted."

"And we do not," the dragon growled. "Freedom of this kind of flight is our birthright and yours." With that, she soared toward the Jungfrau, seeming quite at home in this world of ice and thin air.

"What is your name?" Fírinne wondered out loud. Though this dragon was an old acquaintance, she had always respected the tradition of allowing a dragon to offer its name. "Names hold power," the dragon whispered, with a rush of hot breath that melted a mountainside, sending rocks crashing toward the valley below.

"I meant no offense!" Fírinne quickly corrected herself. "This journey only makes me wonder."

This high, well above the tree line, there were few climbers and no local flora or farms to have been damaged by the dragon-induced avalanche.

Fírinne sighed with relief, turning her attention to the heights surrounding her. She remembered warnings about giddiness at high altitude, as those unused to the rarefied gifts of ice and air often partake of too much too quickly. She checked herself for physical and emotional signs of imbalance, as her memories merged with the view from great height.

The dragon circled lower, allowing her to see, once again, life in these alpine regions. She felt the grinding movement of earthworms far below, and wondered if they were the dragons of the soil. Their presence felt as valuable and necessary as that of the land, the sky, and the cows that thrive on the flora of these holy mountains.

As she descended further, ice became forests and meadows full of flowers. Nature and humans working together in this world of wood and falling water made her heart sing. If only this harmony could be preserved everywhere!

The wavering tones of alp horns drifted through the air. They lulled Fírinne almost to sleep as the undulations of her dragon mount flowed smoothly through the peaks and valleys of her sight and her memories.

"Awakening is an odd business," mused Fírinne, not quite asleep. "After lifetimes of wrapping consciousness around objects of experience and labeling those concepts, my conscious mind suddenly opened and widened with this journey, making those nuggets of knowing obsolete. It feels like too much, too fast. If all of my known perspectives drop away, how will I recognize what I see?" She felt the Amethyst threads of the full moon's infusion weaving a new way of looking at herself and the world around her. Their fluid network and lenses of perception were filled with Grace.

And then, it happened. The dragon on which she rode dove through gathering clouds and into a pasture. Seizing an unsuspecting cow in her jaws, she climbed high once more. Fírinne watched in horror as the dragon made a meal of an innocent beast others held as central to their lives. She felt the

Hathors' laughter as she forced herself not to gag. Beings whose very existence reflects the milk and honey of creation found this massacre funny?

As she struggled with the image and the smell, a memory popped up from childhood. "Why does the cat eat the cute little mice?" she had asked her teacher. The wise woman laughed in answer. "You eat steak," she said. "Mice are cat steaks. Earth is a strange world. You'll get used to it."

Grasping at her courage and the dragon's neck, Fírinne remembered to breathe and trust the light within before she could become horrified by her ego's response to being unmasked. She remembered her teacher's voice, "You will see the horror mirrored in different types of reflections. The first images you will recognize are those actively purging from your field. All unmasking happens this way, at first, because these illusions are more familiar."

An infusion of Hathor energy wrapped its loving tendrils around her heart. "Oh, thank you," she whispered. "This is challenging! I don't understand this shift in perception."

"It is always a challenge when we acknowledge parts of ourselves we would rather deny or take for granted," the Hathors laughed lightly. "The energy of this area is so pure, so clean. Why would the dragon not want to ingest it? Why would you deny yourself such nourishment?"

Fírinne shook her head to clear the sight and odors of what she judged as horrific. Yet, as the dragon fed, she felt satisfaction welling up from within their combined energies. The feeling rose and expanded as the dragon she rode expressed great joy. There was honor in this, of another kind.

Racing into an upward spiral, the dragon roared, "I am the

Matriarch Dragon. I am a ferocious aspect of the Great Mother. I am called by many names. When you allow me in, I am a part of your heart. Let go of your fear. Embrace me."

The embrace of the Hathor vibration held Fírinne steady, and merged with the dragon's roar as they flew. Fírinne's emotions and stomach churned. She feared losing her grip on her mount and, perhaps, her reality.

What sacred cows of perception are you ready to surrender?
What ideas and beliefs about your nourishment are now obsolete?

"I see," Fírinne whispered to Source, gulping down her horror and embracing the nourishment offered by its release. "What else must I relinquish?"

Every single part of this world is being rapidly forced to realign. What is coming cannot be lived from lower vibrations.

Source's voice was simultaneously comforting and terrifying, rising from depths Fírinne had not known existed. She felt her entire being dissolve, much as it had when her body transitioned from its caterpillar consciousness into that of a butterfly. She had known then, in no uncertain terms, that the life of a butterfly is transitory. It was a glad thing; a moment of joy.

"Bring this home," the voice of the dragon encouraged.

"Yes," Fírinne agreed. "I don't know what I am saying yes to, but I will not deny this new nourishment." Quaking with inner realignment, she relinquished her hold on the dragon's neck. As she fell, she felt herself awakening within a realigned body. Cold. She felt cold. It was a bit of energetic shock, she supposed.

Then, after she caught her breath, she bowed a deep bow toward the retreating dragon. She knew the Matriarch Dragon had not retreated permanently, but was allowing her the space to integrate a vast realm of new understanding.

"Home is here, and I carry it with me," Fírinne whispered, touching her heart as she rose on shaky legs to find a cup of tea.

June

The Strawberry Moon ~ Moonstone

I t was almost June! Despite her joy in the revelations received so far, this was a much-anticipated lunation. The strawberry moon of June always promised magic and new light. This moon, the full moon before the June Solstice, is traditionally known for its expansiveness and the harvest season for strawberries. Fírinne knew it as a full moon of great deliciousness.

Strawberries' short harvest season was a delicious reminder to be present and enjoy the gifts of the moment. These juicy red gems had been a favorite for as long as Fírinne could remember. And, as her other-life memories had begun to return, that was a long time indeed.

Taking a bowl from the kitchen, Fírinne stepped outside, just before sunrise, to grab what berries she could. A few birds and one rabbit vacated the strawberry patch just as she approached. "I will leave you some," she promised. As she gently gathered her treasures, something gleamed in the soil under her fingers. "That's where it went!" A small Moonstone pendant she thought had been lost winked at her, waiting. "Hello, you," she smiled as she gathered it up as well.

Moonstone was stepping up as an ally, that was clear. Fírinne was happy to have this little friend with her again. She loved its milky iridescent quality that seemed to shift with the energies needed.

Its relaxing yin energies spoke to depths opening in Fírinne's heart, enhancing her intuitive flow. The soft glow from this stone moved into her heart as compassion and a furthering of ascended empathy.

The more integration she allowed, the more she became willing to trust her abilities and take a chance. She remembered one Rinpoche's instructions to face whatever fear might arise. She knew facing her fears was half the battle, and every time she did so, she realized that the doubt or fear was all in her head.

She felt no fear at this time. At least, she felt nothing like any flavor of fear she had experienced before. With every fiber of her being, she knew that what was coming would expand her horizons in infinite ways. She touched the Moonstone pendant around her neck, grateful for its support.

She had done the research, both inwardly and outwardly. The mystical meaning of the June 2023 Strawberry Moon was an illumination of truth. It was time for her to face the light within and let it shine like the Moonstones she wore to honor this lunation.

The full moon was to occur at 13 degrees of Sagittarius, the sign representing the constellation of the archer whose bow fires the arrow of truth. The frequency of the number 13 holds multi-life lessons and is said to be the numeric herald of Death or Transition, depending on one's point of view. Thirteen is also considered to be the sacred center point of Source, a point of light surrounded by twelve archetypal aspects, gateways, or needed integrations.

Fírinne knew her old world and ways of being were about to die. She had moved through this type of transition many times in this life. "What was one more death and rebirth if it meant an expansion in awareness?"

Just when she had been sure of her unconditional surrender, this alignment arrived to test its mettle. It was time, and she was glad.

Fírinne woke from a lucid dream, taking time only for a quick shower before moving into meditation. A new reality was forming within her visions and dreams. She felt more confident in her perceptions and interpretations than she ever had. "Thanks, Dragon," she sent from her heart as her waking dream continued.

As sparks and currents of light had carried her through the Alps at the last lunation, they now welled up from within the Celtic lands. Natural springs began to flow more freely. Sacred fires, long dormant yet still tended, sprang alight. Those that had not entirely gone out began to burn brightly. A steady warmth rose through every element of earth, sky, and sea. And the land, oh, the feeling that welled up through the soil and stones. These were no bog waters but clear and pristine rising currents of what was to come. The part of her aware of her surroundings sighed in anticipation of physically being on that land.

Her inner vision opened into vast new vistas of perception. The Moonstone resting against her slowly beating heart glowed with the fire of divine connection. As she recognized its vibration, the stones began to sing. Those she wore in her ears chimed lyrically in harmony with the stones on her hand and over her heart. Sitting in meditation, she was drawn into the Solstice opening. She began to feel what she had previously seen as a 3-5 octave rise in frequency delivered by the coming Solstice.

Pure crystalline filaments, ever so delicate yet steely in their tenacity, moved through peak and vale of an emerging continent. Enmeshing their clarities with newly kindled light, they wove new structures before Fírinne's wondering eyes.

The crystalline light filaments became ribbons, currents, and dragon lines held reverently in Gaia's care. Each of these expanded as they all raced into a new cohesion of creation.

"A full moon is a reflection," the cosmos sang. "This is a beginning of fruiting. The fruit needs to fully ripen and drop into your hands - unless it is a strawberry." Fírinne laughed, and remembered her morning foray in the garden, knowing that gathering strawberries took diligence, care and dedication, while leaving just enough for other creatures to enjoy.

"This reflection begins to reveal something about integration and self-inclusion. Huge alignments are present to assist the expansion of awareness. This expansion draws each being into an integrated energy of self-inclusion. What parts of yourself have you not let into your heart? What ripples, what currents of electromagnetic infusion have you yet to recognize and cherish?" The Matriarch Dragon was pulling no punches today.

As this information fired through her mind, Fírinne sank into an emerging vortex of fierce swirling grace. These currents, she knew quite well.

"Rise, dragons! Rise!" she cheered on her kin. Her joy overwhelmed all but the inner spark of light she guarded so closely. Was there now room for more?

What might this new platform be, and how would it manifest physically? Fírinne kept hearing phrases in meditation, like "nothing you might have expected" or "completely different than anything you know." She nodded at Source's whisper.

Wait and see.

Welling up within her body was a clear liquid light. As she relaxed and let it spread, she felt unconditionally supported and inwardly threshed by a radical wave of accountability.

"Why has no one joined me on this journey? Was that assessment even accurate? Many have applied and tried. I have never been alone, within or without. This passage feels different." Fírinne knew a new playing field awaited her. Source's ever-present voice brought her out of vision and into her waking dream.

Letting go does not mean letting go of love. Release all of its forms and, indeed, its attachments.

"What forms might my new reality take? Would I notice? Would this integration be gradual or happen all at once? What changes awaited new choices?"

Still phasing between vision, memory, and waking, Fírinne's guidance showed her the needed information. Last night when she opened the connecting door to the garage, she was swarmed by hundreds of moths. She had never seen so many little brown things in one place! Keeping her mouth shut to prevent swallowing one, she gently waved them away and headed for the big mechanical door to take out the trash. As the door slowly opened, moths streamed out like disturbed bats exiting a cave. She had to duck to be out of their way. So many!

Two or three of the little pests landed in her hair. She tried to dislodge them gently to give them their freedom, wondering what this manifestation was about.

If she remembered correctly, moth medicine was about hidden judgments and resentments eating away at one's inner peace. It also held transformation, similar to a butterfly. With the incoming Solstice wave, it stood to reason that whatever was no longer needed would sluice away. "Where do I still hold any resentment? What do I still want 'out of my hair?'"

Fírinne rattled the bin to the curb and turned to face the house. "I should have left the light out," she thought as moths continued to circle. She looked at the inner wall of the garage and groaned. A hundred or so moths were clustered against it, many near the door that led inside. "They would go for the light, of course. Am I still holding so much? Is all this mine?"

She felt laughter bubbling up inside her. "A fine mess!" she thought as she vented her exasperation by waving as many little creatures away as she could. That felt familiar. Her mind searched for a childhood memory to explain the feeling but failed. Instead, she recalled her years of training in spirituality and metaphysics. She saw and felt every time others judged her. She felt the weight of her body carrying impossibly high standards as nuggets of resentment. She felt what she thought was anger and then shame.

"No! These emotions are the fastest way to disconnect from Source, and there I will not go!" A feeling of adamant burned through her body and mind. "I was trained for this! I choose its release and all that rides with it!"

Then she felt the dragon's voice reverberating through her. "Enough!" roared the Matriarch Dragon. Her wholehearted laughter rang so loudly Fírinne thought the neighbors might hear. A dragon in suburbia!

"Enough! Where are you still pretending by identifying with something ending?" The dragon's message was clear.

Moths dropped dead all over the house for a week before Fírinne began her physical journey. Despite her best efforts to free them, one or two more moths lay dead in corners and windowsills every morning.

Some energies must change form.

Source's voice rang as clearly as the dragon's had that night in the garage. "There must be something I have not been ready to hear," thought Fírinne. "Otherwise, the message would not be so loud or the mirror so obvious."

Packed and ready, Fírinne sat in silence for a final pre-flight meditation. Physical travel was not so much fun these days. She knew she would likely be exhausted on arrival and wanted to retain the clarity brought by the full moon. She intended to glean every last glimmer of Source's offered essence from this adventure. This time, this passage, was what she had incarnated for, after all. There was just enough time before she had to leave for the airport. "Final meditation?" She heard the thought again. "What might that mean?"

Some energies must change form.

She heard the Rinpoche whisper, "Recognition is liberation."

Little did she know this would be a recognition and ownership of her inner light. Her light? All creative essence belonged to Source. Fírinne had been raised on this truth. She accepted it as a given. And yet she heard her own words echoing through her meditation space as the alarm for her departure began to ring.

"To be an embodiment of Source essence, acting through Source, as Source..."

Those last two words were critical, and she knew it. What was she meant to recall?

Immersion in the Celtic lands had always been a treat, and this time was no exception. As always happened, the minute she set foot on the land, her whole body relaxed into its embrace.

She first passed the turnoff on the drive to reach her accommodations. It was almost dark, as logistics had taken longer than anticipated, and she was rapidly turning into a pumpkin, as her mother used to say. Blowing a kiss to the local dragon, who was studiously ignoring her, she drove toward nourishment and bed. The welcome was palpable, but this was not the time.

One evening, typically grey for that time of year, she felt the call. "Now. Come now." Grabbing her gear, Fírinne piled waterproof jacket and trousers, mac, water bottle, and wellies into her rented car and took off. It was blowing up a storm, but the timing felt perfect. She was confident that the open expanse of the Burren's clints and grykes surrounding the sacred site would give her fair warning of incoming weather.

She had always loved the moonscape-like limestone pavement of the Burren. Clints, oddly shaped blocks of stone, rise above widely varied species of lichen and other flora. Fissures between the rocks, known as grykes, vary between those wide enough to allow local cows to graze and deeply-weathered spaces so narrow they make wandering a challenge for the unwary. The surreal feeling of terrain shaped by water and ice had never failed to move her.

The car park, for what was one of the area's most popular tourist attractions, was almost empty. Brilliant. One couple was doffing wet weather gear and piling into their car. A determined tourist, intent on one last photo, persisted until the first big wet drops pelted down. He grabbed his tripod and ran.

Fírinne donned her waterproof outer layers, except for the wellies, and marched slowly through the entrance to the portal. The gravel approach was not much puddled, and the uneven terrain was tricky even when dry. Her trainers were the more practical choice.

She ventured slowly and reverently onto the platform of water-sculpted limestone clints and grykes, supporting what the signage called a portal tomb. Her friend, the dragon, stopped chasing after the photographer, whose tripod she had been knocking to the ground, and beckoned Fírinne closer.

That image vanished, and an image Fírinne associated with the portal gate swam into view. This image, a stacked zigzag of dragon coils, felt static and much too fixed for the occasion. With that thought, undulations of massive golden-white glow moved beneath her feet. These energy currents filled the entire site, making Fírinne feel unsteady. The intensity of light increased until she could no longer stand.

Glad of her knowledge of this place, she carefully made her way to a stone ledge set a bit above the others. Many saw it as an altar and had left flowers and stones on its surface. These Fírinne brushed to one side as she leaned in to the infusion.

"On my own at this sacred site!" She wasn't sure whether to kneel or jump for joy. "Better not to jump," her body chimed in, considering the uneven footing. That made her laugh, which intensified the energy all the more.

"Relax and enjoy," the dragon's voice boomed from the land.

She felt the increased light, the coils of the swimming dragon, at home in its elements, as though they were her own. Within just a few moments, as abruptly as the light had risen, it eased off.

"Go now," she heard. Not wanting to take advantage of the situation, she stood, letting her body and sight align so she would not twist an ankle as she left.

"Go now," the dragon repeated.

Inclining her head in a slight bow toward the voice, Fírinne turned to make her way back toward the car park. She had taken only two steps when a giant maw appeared before her, rising out of the stone. The dragon's head reared as its massive jaws opened and swallowed her whole.

Engulfed in golden flames, Fírinne felt only love and support as she observed star fields birthed and extinguished around her. The event happened so quickly that she had no time to react. She was swept into a crystalline reality construct deep within unknown dimensions. The precision of its sacred geometry was like nothing she had ever seen or experienced. "Was this the dragon's heart?" She felt the truth even as her mind struggled to find words. She knew, with absolute certainty, she had been absorbed into a higher octave of heart essence.

"Go, now." The dragon and Source commanded as one.

As Fírinne gazed across the pasture, she noticed glowering grey clouds almost overhead. The orange glow chasing those clouds was the sunset. It would be dark, soon, and stormy. She turned, wishing she could fly, and walked steadily to her car. A few fat drops pelted the windscreen as she turned the car toward home.

"Home," she whispered to herself. "Yes." And, as she gathered up her things and opened the front door of the B&B, it began to rain in earnest.

"Aren't you lucky!" her host exclaimed as she entered the lobby. "Did you get caught?"

"No," Fírinne grinned back at him. "Just not." She gestured toward the storm as a lightning flash and thunderous crash shook the front of the building. "Did it hit?" she asked the inn keeper, who was still smiling.

"Just not," he chuckled. Fírinne's grin grew as she found her room and placed her key in the lock with the help of another flash of lightning.

"Now that will take some unpacking," she sang to the cows lying down and sheltering behind the building. "Thanks for holding down the fort." One of her favorites twitched an ear and lowed back at her, filling a pause in the thunderstorm with welcome.

As her days in these lands moved toward their ending, Fírinne spent this precious time exploring a bit further each day, following the download of frequencies. The surge moved west and north, past the Outer Hebrides and into the North Atlantic. Something from deep memory flickered in her heart, awakening and returning. She felt warm currents moving within new tides of light. Was the new construct forming beneath the sea?

July

The Buck Moon ~ Ruby Dragon Glow

Fírinne watched the surge of amplified energy move into the North Atlantic and become hidden beneath its depths. As her plane took off, she felt a new warmth rising to support what was shifting. The North Atlantic had always felt cold to her. Its currents felt supportive, like the sea always felt, yet icy in their depths. But now, a clandestine glow of support permeated the sea floor and the entire Earth's crust. Fed by pristine magmatic elemental energies, its percolating warmth followed Fírinne on her journey home. Gazing out the plane window, she noticed a glow beneath the waves.

Her inner vision perceived clusters of Ruby crystal points, growing larger and larger but veiled, as though seen through filtered glass. Their deep red glow permeated the elements of nature, working clandestinely from every dimension.

As time marched toward the next lunation, rising warmth began to activate Ruby crystals throughout the world. A deep rosy glow came from the Earth's crust, fed by the pristine magmatic elemental energies of fire and water. It reminded Fírinne of childhood sunsets, whose delicate light bathed the world in what she had then called 'pink hope.'

Fírinne set her alarm, rising earlier than usual so that she might see the full moon before it set behind the peaks. Her effort rewarded her with brilliant white light, unobscured by cloud or storm. A kind of silvery daylight bathed the landscape in still, cold mystery. Temperatures soared during this season, yet the moonlight carried the frosty breath of polar winds. Their currents invigorated Fírinne as she took the time to make a pot of tea and settle in for meditation.

The exact alignment occurred at 11 degrees, 18 minutes, of Capricorn, which was significant for several reasons. The sign of Capricorn is all about the practical, our business lives, our career lives, how we manifest things in the physical, and how we go about navigating the structures of our day-to-day. The number 11, the one-one, is considered to be a doorway. For some, it represents ancient pillars in temples more ancient still. Between these pillars of light, we pass through the phases of our lives.

Fírinne held such a doorway in her vision as she moved into meditation. Careful not to project through the opening, she knew it would guide her to what she was meant to see. Clarity of intent was the key to this alignment. She was sure of it, though she was unsure what that meant for her and how it might play out.

Go deeper, she heard Source whisper. *Deeper than ever before.*

Fields of stars surrounded her as she gave herself to vision, and from this infinite embrace emerged a white stag made entirely of pure light. "The magical stag!" she whispered, her voice sounding loud among the stars. "Of course!"

The white stag appeared throughout Celtic legend. Its massive crown of antlers stretched into the heavens; its feet firmly planted as though it drew its existence from Gaia's core. Wherever Fírinne had encountered images of this creature, the pictures had pierced her heart. What incredible essence this magical being held! Kingdoms, physical and non-physical, birthed, died, and were reborn within its crown. One such being had allegedly guided Arthur to find Excalibur.

"Will there be swords involved?" Fírinne wondered, grinning. The stag was not present to lead her, however. It merged with her heart almost instantly, altering her perspective. The fields of stars became the seas of this world. In they went, Fírinne-as-Stag, deep within the embrace of the sea.

"Was 'they' even appropriate?" Fírinne thought, as consciousness raced ahead of her, plunging into the Earth's core.

Converged at the stellar heart of Gaia were countless other beings. An array of lifeforms radiated like spokes from a great wheel, all connected through Gaia's core. From Gaia's crystalline heart, light beamed through each one, filling and illuminating unique filaments of light within every heart. New crystalline fibers activated with each pulse of illumination. All of these beings were connected by, and part of, a vast network of luminescence.

Powerful pulses of plasmic luminosity filled the field of Fírinne's vision, dissolving all sense of self. "Perception simply is," she whispered as her physical consciousness was left behind.

These are the elements of change. The new weave is in place. It is done.

Source's soft, powerful voice permeated the multiverse. Peace and power reverberated through all hearts as one. Fírinne felt a blending of innocence and maturity, drawing her close. Stillness took over, and she was lost to space and time. She drifted through life experience after life experience, watching as each lesson, each jewel of understanding, presented itself and dissolved. Streaming as starlight, she giggled as each life ended and her essence moved on.

As the stag, she ran and leaped between the worlds, allowing herself to receive each precious gift of knowing. With each integration, her joy increased, its lightness almost too much to bear. And then, it seemed there was always more.

A blast of pure white light jolted her into sharply focused awareness. Here was Gaia's heart once more, enveloping all beings as one. The burst of light swallowed each being, transforming them into explosions of spark-like droplets of liquid crystal. Then, these particles of pure light radiated throughout the entire planet. "My planet," Fírinne realized. "My world for now." She had made that commitment somewhere, she remembered, as love for this world gushed through her heart.

Each liquid crystal prism navigated according to its particular resonance: each a gem of absolute pristine discernment. As these particles disseminated worldwide, she watched as a new web of light was woven. What belonged in the new platform would be sustained and supported through this network. What did not belong dissolved or sluiced away.

Fírinne watched this breathtaking event as an external observer, even as she felt her stag-self explode into fluid particles of plasmic grace. The crown of antlers that had adorned the great stag's head now rested within Gaia's heart. Fírinne wondered at the sight even as it made her heart glad.

Gladness welled up through the seas as part of this transformation. She witnessed the revitalization of Ruby crystals throughout the planet. "Ruby crystals? Why did that image keep coming up, and why did it feel familiar?"

Memories from distant learning flowed through her awareness. Ruby crystals had, long ago, been used to amplify creative energies. Some adepts, concerned with the overuse of these mineral allies, removed the Ruby crystals from their laboratories and temples. They asked for the assistance of elemental beings to secret these gems beneath the seas.

What was hidden is reactivating.

In her studies, Fírinne had learned that the stone, Ruby, promotes loving nurturing, health, knowledge, and abundance. It improves energy and aids concentration. It represents creativity, loyalty, honor, and compassion. Ruby's essence can protect and stimulate heart energy and spiritual wisdom.

Star rubies, rubies with a six-rayed pattern at the center, carry the same qualities, but with enhanced healing and magical powers. This stone was said to be the most powerful at a full moon. This was that moon, the buck moon, with enhanced heart energy as its essence.

It was clear that Ruby had stepped up as the ally for this transformation. Fírinne remembered that, in ancient times, Ruby was used to integrate high-frequency energy into the physical body, grounding intense frequencies into wholeness. Having passed through many such integrations, mature adepts often wore it as a reminder of spiritual light. Rather than denoting rank, wearing the Ruby crystal indicated the ability to embody higher octave frequencies with discernment and integrity.

The Buck moon, another name for the full moon of July, was so named for the maturation and flowering of the crown in a male deer. Maturity. Grounding. Wholeness. As each concept rang through her awareness, their constructs changed and became more. She began to know how her world was changing without needing to understand. This knowing carried and supported the voice of the Stag.

"New cycles of maturity beckon with each round of molting and growing. More wisdom flows within me as my crown reaches for the light. This wisdom I carry lightly, as all things are made of light." The essence of the white stag embodied spiritual wisdom in a grounded way. His voice completed an understanding in

Fírinne's heart. And with that flash of claircognizance, she passed into and through the offered gateway.

This lunation occurred within the gateway of '11,' at 11 degrees of the sign of Capricorn. She had learned that the number eleven was not only a doorway but the archetype of Justice in the tarot. This memory accelerated her progress, drawing her into currents of fairness, truth, and sacred law. The doorway presented by the 11th degree was a slipstream, allowing one to be pulled through and out of all old-world entanglements. She had learned that Sacred law was all about alignment as the truth of being. Nature was the best, perhaps the only, example of this revered alignment. Seemingly entangled only within itself, Nature remained forever sustainably aligned. This truth, Fírinne remembered well.

Her attention was drawn to the conceptual architecture of Justice. She knew that the Egyptian Goddess Ma'at often represented the divine feminine aspect of Justice. Her wings symbolize the freedom of a balanced heart. In one hand, she holds the scales of Divine Justice, upon which hearts are weighed against a feather. She illuminates the practice of lightening the heart. Divine Justice is not blind at all. She embodies clarity of perception. With this discernment, she can truly see.

The light that had just burst through Gaia's heart now radiated through Fírinne's. Lightness of heart vibrated intensely through her body. Joy was its manifestation.

This lightness is the percolating heart essence that will fuel further transformation.

"I am surrendering heaviness of heart," Fírinne realized, as Source's voice reverberated through every cell and fiber. And, as the realization flowed through her, it redirected her focus to the Ruby crystals. They grew larger and larger but still shadowed, as though seen through a glass, darkly. "Does that saying come from an understanding of filtered perception?" Fírinne wondered. With that thought, a surge of crystalline plasma tipped her inner balance into the realms of the dragon's heart, remembered from the last lunation.

"New realms of heart. Yes." Fírinne's mind could not supply words or data fast enough to keep up with this majestic architecture of sacred geometry. Its pure, prismatic reflections were part of this transmission, designed to reactivate the Ruby crystals worldwide and in every body.

The keys to grounding this activation were discernment and clarity. "Resonance determines everything," Fírinne recalled. Inner light is intelligence. It knows what to do. It designs every essence to morph accordingly.

Plasmic crystals of light began to bond with Ruby wherever that form existed. Fírinne watched as various Ruby crystals began to glow, to grow, and some to dissolve completely. Those that were lighting up shone from within. She noticed that the flow of light crystals seemed to ignore some forms and navigate toward others. Source's guiding hand was palpably present as this new network within the Flower of Life began to form.

A dragon of pure Ruby essence emerged from deep within the elemental realms and moved through Fírinne's field of attention. Its scales appeared to be made of gems, glowing with the light of its inner fire. It circled around and through her until she felt individuated once again.

The Ruby Dragon spoke then, just once, as Fírinne's awareness reformed.

"We dragons of the energetic deep reside within the realms of what humans call 'magic.' I surface now to remind you of what you are becoming. Be clear on what resonates with you and what does not. Let your Source Essence create your new path. Know that such a path forms beneath the willing steps of courageous feet. Do not waver. Our love is always with you."

With that, the Ruby Dragon plunged into Gaia's heart, trailing glowing sparks of stellar fire. "Was there an opening there? It seemed so. What if one dragon's heart held an opening to all the others?"

Fírinne's heart raced as she became increasingly aware of her body and surroundings. She could almost see a rosy glow coming from her hands as she held them up in front of her.

All is in place. A new age of maturation has begun.

As often happened when Source's voice sounded through her field, Fírinne began to weep. Tears of joy flooded her eyes, ran down her face, and amplified the rosy glow from her hands.

"Liquid love," she gasped, oh so softly. "Am I ready for the fluidity and power of real love?"

At that, the Matriarch Dragon, the guide for her Solstice flight, chuckled softly. "There, there, little one. Don't grasp too far ahead. Your metamorphosis has only begun."

Curling her body into a fetal ball, Fírinne let her awareness bask among the stars.

August

Grain Moon, Lynx Moon ~ Fire Quartz

Altitude sun burned hot on her back as Fírinne stood on a local path in full view of the mountains. She had wandered out, later than usual, to tap in to the upcoming full moon. Noon sun blasted through sheltering treetops, threatening to crisp their leafy canopy before Autumn's seasonal changes painted them in fiery colors. Today was hot. And August was still a few days away. There would be two full moons this coming month, each promising another dive into facing one's fears and letting them burn.

Fírinne faced the fire walk that August represented with more curiosity than fear. It felt like the Ruby Dragon had melted into the planet or had, at least, gone into stealth mode far beneath the surface. Its essence percolated within Gaia's mantle and crust as a gorgeous rosy glow. Wherever Fírinne cast her inner sight, she felt the immensity of the dragon's heart. It held and moved through the earth's crust and the green world, the skies and the seas. Even the buildings and highways rippled with a new intensity.

Queen of the elemental realms, the Ruby Dragon often hid in plain sight. She could be felt in every blossoming, every harvest, and every seasonal shift. Fírinne was grateful to have been introduced to such a magnificent being and to have such powerful guidance. She wondered what shape its integration would take.

That this was a time of deep gestation of what was to come was as obvious as obvious gets. She wondered where to begin this next phase of her journey and heard,

This happens in awareness. This leg of your journey happens inside yourself.

With that knowing, Fírinne felt somehow lighter and relieved, as though a great weight had lifted. It was Gaia's journey, after all. She, like all bipeds, was simply along for the ride.

It had taken days for her body to integrate the last lunation's energies. This new infusion felt massive in comparison. What was now to come? Source's voice was, again, unmistakable.

Be still. Open and receive.

"I am only privileged to observe and witness, and hopefully, transform." The truth of that knowing lifted her spirits even as her body sank further into transitioning energies. Part of her wanted to go outside, be with nature, re-connect with the dragon energies, and feel what was happening so far beneath all surfaces. Her body, however, had other ideas. It wanted to rest, gestate, and integrate at the cellular level. Realizing this, she understood that the Ruby Dragon, at least, was part of her now. That realization made her smile, the slow lazy smile reserved for cozy kitchens and summer afternoons.

Fírinne remembered this feeling in her body as a heaviness, a reluctance to engage with the world, and something that deserved her focused attention. "Observe and learn," she reminded herself as she curled up with a cup of tea. Others were out enjoying high summer. She smiled a lynx-like knowing smile as she felt them go about their ways.

Leaning ever more deeply into her inner Silence, she asked her body to be open to receive new infusions and information as it came. With that, she let go and let vision take her.

She allowed her mind to review stored information regarding this full moon. What were its particulars? Was there anything she needed to remember? Perhaps she could at least begin to feel what her mind could not yet grasp. With calm anticipation, she looked forward to what the lunation might reveal. Breathing out to calm her heart she looked inward. This was going to be intense.

The first full moon of August occurred on the 1st day, at 9 degrees Aquarius. A Goddess number in an air sign, this alignment would contribute claircognizance to infusions of knowing, and invoke the Goddesses of the Grain, Persephone and Ceres, whose archetypal forms herald the arrival of abundance.

Fírinne recalled the teachings of Persephone, who chose to exit the underworld not by any external permission, but by raising her arms as the Goddess she is, exposing her winged heart. Then, with one circular motion, she shape-shifted the world around her, exiting the underworld and creating a new, ripening, surface world.

Fírinne felt the warmth and power of this abundance of creation, and saw the image of Ceres, a sheaf of ripened grain in her pristinely white arms. Her Mother Goddess frequencies sang of nurturing, comfort and care.

"This full moon is all about abundance, reflected in the warm heart and cool head of the sun-moon alignment." Was it Ceres or Persephone who spoke? Fírinne could not tell. "Discernment is amplified with this alignment," she heard deep within her heart. "Deep discernment is needed in taking next steps," she realized.

"Much-needed clarity would enter the arena of transformation during this lunar infusion. Inner fire, combined with inner alignment, would ultimately produce inner wisdom. The Source

Essence of each being on the planet was lighting up. This would be a time of release and relief." Fírinne felt her shoulders relax as that information took hold.

She remembered that the August full moon could be known as the grain moon, and sometimes the lynx moon. That memory captured her attention. Her relaxed gaze moved to the spirit lynx on her wall. What a companion it had become. While the grain moon represents abundance in the form of first harvest, a gathering of promise and potential, the lynx, as an ally, represents the holder of secrets. Its antennaed ears represent clairaudience. Its stealthy ways allow it to perceive what is often ignored or misrepresented. How were the Goddesses of the grain and the lynx related as part of this cycle? What were their roles in the weave?

"Secrets hold a harvest in and of themselves." Of course. Threads of lynx medicine wrapped around an inner cornucopia of all she had learned, binding it close within her. The wealth it contained was priceless, to be sure. What was it worth to her? "Everything." So spoke her inner truth.

"This inner re-alignment has everything to do with how we take responsibility for our own energy; not whether we take responsibility, but how." The memories of her training continued. It has everything to do with integrity and discernment and how that flows from the Galactic Mother's heart and my own. These qualities are the pillars of an inner temple built within my physical body. Wisdom in the construction of this temple is rooted in how I allow myself to think. What diet am I feeding my mind? What can be released, freed from my mind's clutching grasp?

"This lunation is all about abundance and discernment. What could be more nurturing to re-constructing a mind? Am I becoming a more optimal configuration? Is that possible on this world at this time?" Fírinne knew she was onto something, but knew not what. An open inner query took her deeper into the mystery. What was about to be revealed?

Fire Quartz stepped up as holder of this infusion of transforming energies as if in answer. This form of quartz represents the fire that lives inside everyone. "I aid all beings in recognizing and practicing their abundantly available inner strength. My power can reignite the embers one needs to persevere."

"Perfect," Fírinne breathed, as vision took her beyond the known and into the realm of potentials and possibilities.

At one point in her mystical training, Fírinne had spent her nights in the same room as a tall Fire Quartz crystal. Its energy seemed to encourage her as she learned to meditate and discern her body's need for sleep. She was taught that this powerful crystal can help manifest desires and create a smooth pathway, or conduit, for higher levels of consciousness to travel through. These circuits, currents, or threads focused the inner reclamation of her magical essence, her energy that understands what lives beyond images and words. "I need that now," she whispered. "Thank you for reminding me."

She felt timelines and trajectories open up with the rising of the moon. Not yet ready to be traversed, each glistened with potential. The full moon's light reflected worlds ready to be explored. Deep threads, gleaming like bits of silver wire, appeared in her physical body. No longer connected to the present or the past, these bits of rigid material rose to the surface of her awareness like flotsam to be gathered and then swept away.

Fírinne sensed that attention was the required currency for this act of re-creation. Dropping completely into the function of observer, she watched her inner landscape alter.

Threads   unraveled,   creating   virgin   inner   territory   by relinquishing their lacings of control. "The deepest weaves of my survival programs are surfacing to be surrendered," she realized. "As this internal wiring dematerializes, the parts of me it has held together for so long feel a little bereft, abandoned, and fragile. These parts feel like wet cement with no reinforcement, or bamboo scaffolding, without lacings to tie it in place. What is truly mine will be distilled into golden nuggets of truth. What does not belong to me and my further journey will melt away."

Fírinne felt the embers of germination along with the meltdown of every flavor of distortion. "Some clarity through the chaotic energies would help," she whispered to the Source inside her.

August 6-7-8 holds the Lion's Gate alignment this year. "Most people will be focused on the 8:8," she mused. "Good! Maybe the disparity will give me a clear shot at perceiving." Psychic empath that she was, Fírinne had trained to discern genuine insights from the cacophony of collective thought and imagination. Much of her early training had focused on this.

"Notice the thoughts, the thought patterns. Do not engage any. Do not follow any story but that emerging through you." Her teachers had been adamant about this. "If you feel a thought pattern or story in your body, listen. Are those thoughts originating from you or from somewhere else?"

"But how do I tell?" she had initially protested. "You will learn," was the response. "You will know by how it feels in your integrated core."

She remembered curling into a fetal ball, huddled close against the energies swirling around her. She welcomed the memory of her confused toddler self into Source's arms as she rested, gratefully, in an orb of light. "Those boundaries are now held by Source," she smiled. "What a journey this has been. Have I matured from what I have learned? What new learning will this transformation bring? I must relax and let Source inform my expression, thoughts, and vibrational choices. If all lenses of perception are undergoing radical alteration, how will I perceive the truth?"

The child she had been was afraid to see what swirled around her. Now, Fírinne could hardly wait.

This lunation lit new fires. What new presence will now be forged?

"This is a completion of everything that has been distracting me from what is ready to be built within me. It is dissolving anything that has been in the way." That thought summoned the Ruby Dragon from her dissolution games beneath the seas.

"Fly with me," she commanded. Her glowing form rippled through rock and waves, carrying Fírinne's awareness at lovespeed. Newly created lines of luminosity threaded through the mineral and aquatic realms. Infinite in their numbers, they formed exquisite designs. Each pattern flowed and changed as the dragon merged with it and moved on. Where there might have been a tangle or possible enmeshment, the dragon's passage smoothed the way.

Mesmerized by the light play, Fírinne could only observe its fiery dance. And then, an infusion of moonlight laced with fire entered her vision. She felt the dragon's heart, illuminated by this glowing ember, intertwined with All That Is. Held in the dragon's heart space, she relaxed further into the rising light.

The heart is the first gateway. You know this to be true.

Source's voice altered everything. Here was the direct transmission at last.

This is an abundant lunation of honoring inner light. A deeper heart activation has not yet occurred in your lifetime.

This is a lunation of absolute, Source-level freedom. The liberation that will form throughout Gaia will vary according to the particle, or being, it encounters. What does freedom mean? What do you believe is possible? This is most definitely a fire alignment due to the portal you are traversing. Events in the physical world reflect that. When the outer world is on fire, what does that reflection tell you about your heart?

Heart portals are opening up all over the world. Will you be one of them? Will you bring that energy with you wherever you go?

Fírinne felt a whirlpool of energy opening beneath her. Its churning spiral glistened with every imaginable color. She felt increasingly calm as the light pulled her in, setting her old storyboards on fire. "What might this new chapter bring?" She felt ready.

No. Not yet.

Source's voice had never sounded so adamant. Images of threshing floors, a massive cornucopia of blessings that turned into a colossal sorting hat, and transformations of every kind filled her sight. The chaos was too much for her mind to handle. She could only release all of herself deeper and deeper into the swirling light, trusting that stability would find her. Then she remembered the dragon's heart, and that she was adrift within its embrace.

Suddenly, a burst of light filled Gaia's center. Waves radiated from the blast in every direction. 'A planetary spherical morphing wave,' thought Fírinne. "Will there be more than one pulse? Is this...?" Her thoughts stopped as the tide moved through her body and mind.

She remembered the first orbs of Pearl and Sapphire. Their

infusions had seemed strong, but her current experience of this lunation and its transformations were obliterating everything that had gone before.

Your old world is gone. The new waits on threads of choice.

"I know there is a true alignment that changes, morphs, and shifts constantly. It is very fluid. This is the 'I am' within me. It is what I have been, and always will be. It is a configuration of Source essence. This particular lunation invites all beings into their own fluid alignment in ways unique to each of them. I choose to trust this with all that I am." Fírinne had never felt so committed or so blessed. Dissolved into sparkles of light, yet cohesive in her energy body, she knew this place and was known. And, with that knowing came immersion in the Great Mother's love.

The heart has always been the primary gateway beyond the illusions of this world. Now, at this time of transition, it is the only way.

She felt an ember of light growing within the dragon's heart and her own. The more her old stories fell away the more light fed this gestation. "The new frequency bundle is manifesting through me," she realized. "It will not be noticeable in the life around me until I have become it." Distortions she had not imagined possible melted before her inner sight until she was almost afraid to open her eyes. What would be left of any reality whatsoever?

Knowing better and mustering her courage, she asked again for clarity.

What remains is the heart.

"Most people won't know what that means," she said out loud.

"You are not 'most people,'" the dragon replied. "Become this. You will know so that others might see. Embody this change and let it emanate from within you, that others may perceive it within themselves.

Let yourself morph. Feel the shifts and changes without trying to make mental sense of them. As your essence is distilled, you will dissolve again and again into your purest, most crystalline frequencies. From there, new worlds will be born." Wisdom pulsed through the heart of the dragon.

"When will this be complete? Will my allies change? What is yet to be revealed?" Fírinne's mind was getting the better of her, despite herself and her lifetimes of training. It felt like she was coming apart at the seams. That made no sense to her expanded awareness, so she laughed and chose to let go. Turning fully inward, though that direction made no sense at the moment, she listened.

"You have prepared for this," growled the voice of the Matriarch Dragon. "Let us, and all of your allies, assist you in your Great Remembering."

Fírinne's sight flooded with images of crystalline forms being swapped in and out of her various bodies. Silencing her mind, she watched as higher octaves of light and sound entered and integrated into her signature configuration. Her bundle of light filaments grew and changed. The process merged and dissolved every one of her mental images into Oneness. "This is what it is to 'be.'"

She knew this feeling, and her physical body relaxed. Exhaling deeply, she gave herself to the light. Fírinne let her individuated awareness move entirely into flow, resting in the feeling of the dragon's taloned paws supporting each of her shoulders.

She leaned into the dragon's body, feeling the vast tail rocking them both on Source's waves of change. As they traveled, she was absorbed within the Matriarch Dragon's heart. Whereas it had initially appeared as a geometric prism of light, the vast space now had content. High-frequency infusions nourished its expanded state. Fírinne felt totally reborn and nurtured as a cohesive soft gem of stellar emanation.

What had been a human body, with its patterns and identifications, now glowed with an incandescent flame. Any clarity she had been pursuing seemed childish and irrelevant. She blinked inside the golden-white light, like an infant waking from a deep sleep.

"Rest, for now," the Matriarch Dragon softly growled. And, with that, the dragon vanished. In her place gleamed a lynx-like chimera of golden secrets. Fírinne was left to ponder the nature of this ember of amber light, as she began to integrate the deepest essence of herself.

August's Second Moon

Amber Tides of Change

Like purifying Amber, every inclusion in Fírinne's meltdown disappeared. Bits and pieces of herself and her experiences floated to the surface and burned off. The translucent Amber-like nugget of warmth and peace from the last lunation began fully integrating into her body and awareness. She had been enjoying the depths of the meltdown, the honeyed flow of ancient wisdom into a formless form, fed by stellar light.

Deep, deep closure echoed through her body and mind. "This is it, this is it, this is what I incarnated for," framed the joy accompanying every surge of transformation. "I keep saying that," she grinned. "And there are four more lunations to follow this one. I can't see past the Equinox in September. It looks like another explosion of light. I had better not get ahead of things, though."

The moon's bright disk, not yet full, had not entirely set behind the mountains. The brisk mountain air had the beginnings of an Autumn tang. Fírinne had missed the smell of new fires and falling leaves. Fox and coyote bounded off at her approach, avoiding human contact in the quiet of their early morning rounds. The sight of them always warmed Fírinne's heart. The mountain range, whose grounding she sought, loomed ahead. As she rounded a corner and left the neighborhood behind, the highest peaks and setting moon began to glow pink with the rising sun. Lovely! "This is just what I need," she whispered. "No matter what else is obliterated, you remain." She plopped onto a convenient bench, letting the mountains' morning blessing wash over her.

"This lunation dissolves even the most trusted distillations of belief for me and the world. How are others faring? It must be confusing and bring up hidden terrors for those less conscious. Anyone can see that even in the depths of collective denial, what was is no longer."

As the moon disappeared, the sun rose. Heat and intensity followed it. Fírinne paused under an obliging tree before returning home to meditate. "Oh, blessed green world. Thank you for your support and guidance." She could almost hear the dryads giggling as fading blossoms cascaded over her. "Thanks for not tossing the berries!" she grinned. With one last look at the heights of the Continental Divide, she turned for home. 'Here we go,' she sent from her heart.

This is a completion. All is in place for the new that now needs to gestate. The field has been cleared. And now, it begins.

Fírinne heard Source's voice more clearly than ever before, though the messages felt odd in her blenderized field. Her discernment was more precise. She felt rather than heard, seeing the light etchings of each energy encountered. Her knowing felt complete, even as it morphed and shifted.

She rested like a distilled nugget of Amber washed into the sunlight on a pristine shore. Her heart radiated the warmth of the snugly banked embers of a winter fire. Every part of her reveled in a new glow. Some part of her knew to enjoy this while it lasted. And she did.

These are the deep tides of change. The nugget you perceive yourself to be is liquefying into its purest essence.

"Amber," thought Fírinne. "Amber volunteered to become an ally through the obliteration of all old ways of being. Long considered a gem in ancient traditions, its distilled essence of the green world's life force was the embodiment of total transformation." She knew Amber's ancient origins vary from a million to over 300 million years. Initially a sticky, semi-liquid tree resin, hardens by losing parts of itself, evaporating into the air over a few days to a few years. "A bit like me," Fírinne chuckled.

During the second stage of solidifying, the resin molecules polymerize, linking with each other to form larger molecules. The process can take several tens of thousands to millions of years. Within each nugget of Amber reside the ancient wisdom and the cumulative stellar downloads of its passage into solid form.

"Am I like that? Truly? Wouldn't that be a wonder?" Fírinne had always wondered about Amber. It always held magic for her. It was the first gem she had fallen in love with long ago, in her first Teacher's house. As a toddler, she had stealthily taken the mala made of round golden beads from her Godmother's table and poured it through her tiny hands. The beads sang to her listening heart while she ought to have been napping, providing delicious rest.

When caught, finally asleep, with the beads clutched in tender hands, her Godmother asked one thing only. "What do they tell you?" Fírinne giggled with joy at being understood completely.

Her Godmother, also her first Teacher, told her that, in its gem form, Amber is a record-keeper for the inner evolution of our world. These nuggets have been revered throughout history for their emanations of steadiness and support, due to the bright, soothing energy that can help calm the nervous system and balance the brain. Little Fírinne didn't know what that meant but trusted that she would in time.

She knew, in her heart, that Amber's essence feeds the wisdom held in embodied sacred space. Somehow, it fed her Godmother as it fed her dreams.

Her adult mind and heart began to remember more. Amber can assist with tissue revitalization and physical vitality as one learns to become sacred space. It is a unique gem in that it can float yet is harder than other resins. It embodies the inner toughness and courage required for total transformation. Amber is a key to ancient knowledge and can stimulate the remembrance of lineage, genetic lessons, and experiences passed on from galactic ancestors. All this Fírinne remembered, glad once more for her years of study and training. As challenging as those years had been, she was so very grateful.

One of the treasures Fírinne kept from the lives that had dissolved around her was a strand of Baltic Amber. She bought it for herself as an awakening gift. Its electrically charged essence drew her across a conference floor crowded with stalls filled with merchandise and had almost bounced up and down on the vendor's table. "Me! I want to come with you!" Fírinne had put it about her neck then and there, and its presence had assisted her with many of her Priestess functions, especially when she needed to ground higher frequencies.

The necklace was a dear friend whose support now meant more than ever. She began to wear it daily as the month's gestation proceeded. "Comfort and joy," it seemed to say. Did she have any idea what those qualities of life could be? Fire Quartz had been a stalwart ally, feeding the flames of dissolution. Amber fed another source of nourishment, nurturing, and cherishing. It felt like wearing or becoming the heart of a dragon.

Being drawn into the Matriarch Dragon's heart, as she had at the last lunation, Fírinne had tried to respect that gift by letting it instruct her in its own way. Exploring the honeycomb of the dragon's heart in meditation had replaced most other forms of engagement. Each time Fírinne relaxed into its glowing golden light, the dragon guided her into another realm. 'How many chambers does a dragon's heart have?' she wondered.

"I am an infinite being. What limits might there be?" was the answer. "The entirety of you is shifting into the currents of the water rabbit year, deepening into the mystery and the magic of the dance of form and formlessness that you are. Remember that this is a world of learning through immersion. Let your 'self' go."

The closer the full moon came, the more of Fírinne melted away. Just when she thought no more could be distilled, the morphing continued.

The dragon's voice thrummed through Fírinne's reality, changing it with every breath. She recognized the framework, the details, the packaging of this life, and what she had agreed to experience. More than that, she saw the entire landscape of her lifetime. The dragon's perspective showed her the original intent and design for learning from ovum/seminal imprinting, the patterns that her body's conception set in motion, and how that had played out thus far. She felt, saw, and knew the repeating loops of her life as currents in a more significant tide of wisdom. And now, they were obsolete. All that she had lived within was no more.

Fírinne recognized herself as an image, a space-time pixel of promise. She saw through her avatar status in a learning paradigm of sound and light and laughed at the truth of the avatar masks used online. How much effort and energy she had put into an image to hide behind! She knew, without question, what had integrated into this space-time pixel and what no longer resonated. Her nugget of Amber glowed with peace, discernment, and empowerment.

She saw the breadth and depth of what she had agreed to learn as she saw the structures of her lessons and whence they came. She watched in growing joy as those storyboards burned.

The house her life had built had been gone for a long time. More walls had dissolved with each awakening. Her old stories had remained, though, like wallpaper, first faded and torn, then becoming more and more transparent until they gleamed like etchings on the ethers. But now, those illusory boundaries were no more. Life beyond limitation. What would that be like?

There had been the work of moving through patterns and programs of transcendence. It had been her life's work. This was different. This was freedom beyond the boxes her life had been lived within. She honored the illusion of her life, even as the winds of change made art in the ethers from her ashes.

She saw and felt the buried wiring of her dependency on patriarchal principles. Fear and terror surfaced as remnants of primal scream ripped through her tissues. The demise of those systems had to happen within her heart before she became free. She felt the Matriarch Dragon supporting her as hidden fears became known and dissipated.

With each recognition and release, a wave of mounting joy became almost more than she could bear. Fírinne repeatedly retreated into nature, as only its harmony made sense in this riot of constant transformation.

Gazing heavenward, she watched as geese and raptors circled the skies. Their energy signals joined those of the dragons, shaping the clouds above her head. She felt their paths as though swizzle sticks of light darted from each winged one and plunged through her body, intersecting at her sacral center, connecting her with the flights of each bird and with Gaia's core beneath her feet. Birdsong and the voices of the trees and grasses blended into nature's symphony, vibrating the ground on which she stood.

Bliss? Ecstasy? Joy? Though she had experienced these uplifted states before, they paled in the face of what was expressed through her body and being. The dragons' voices blended into the amplification of sacred sound, absorbed into that of the Matriarch Dragon, at last. "You have completed what you agreed to learn."

"Does that mean I'm finished here?" she wondered.

"Only if you desire to be," whispered the Matriarch Dragon. "This transit is a powerful window of closure on the structures of an old life. This is the completion of a particular cycle of love."

It was a particular cycle of love. That last made her shiver. She felt the truth of it right down to her bone marrow, lifting her into new octaves of light. Eagle, hawk, owl, and falcon taught her their knowledge of thermal riding and soaring as a means of navigation and play. She had read, long ago, about rising to find the meaning of living as love. Was this that wisdom? How did a healed heart come into play?

How can lifetimes of heartbreak be transmuted? This was part of what she had incarnated to learn. It seemed that physical bodies held the keys. What was now released or held happened through physical form. Her body was melting. All of its patterns and programmed responses dropped away. She felt a small part of her wondering what that would mean and if there was any reason to remain in this world. The Matriarch Dragon indicated that staying was a choice to play as the new currents and flows of light.

Earth school. Could Earth School become a playground? Maybe it had always been. It had always helped Fírinne's reactive sense to remember that this lifetime is one of learning and transformation. Nothing is meant to endure but the truth. And this was a Pisces full moon. It melded a fire reset with tidal waves of integration. As the moon rose, new tides rose with it.

An alchemy of fire and water begins.

This lunation held a shift in the foundations of support. The astronomical facts and figures, the numerology of the change, had all become like sand in Fírinne's mouth. None of the infinite grains of metaphysical knowledge she had learned seemed to matter. When an entire paradigm is obliterated, what is there to retain, record, or defend? What facts could possibly stand up to this great truth?

Moonlight bathed her journal as she began translating her experience into words. It was a strange sensation to put pen to paper. Fírinne's hands shook as she began to write. Questions and answers formed themselves on the page. What will be mine to inhabit? Will everyone begin to see life in new ways? Each will look through the lens of a different kind of habitation. It is not only bodies that are changing but how each body is inhabited. Rather than looking at what needs to dissolve, that lens has dissolved completely.

She surrendered into the flow of information, and as she did so, the writing became more manageable. She could hear the voice of the Matriarch Dragon more easily.

"You are asked to let the inner space created by this burning and gestating fill up with higher frequencies of light and love. All old structures are only taking up space now needed for new embodiment. You will feel formless at this time, primarily. You must let any discomfort go and let all that love, peace, power, and purity fill you up. As your distortions dissolve, you cannot help but perceive differently. Gone are the old external support systems that contained sabotage at their cores. Those courses have been completed or canceled. That school of learning is most definitely over."

"How fluid will perception become? This moon is a massive opportunity to observe how morphable life is." The pen dropped from Fírinne's hand as her thoughts raced on.

"Humans are like infants who have not yet learned how to be supported in the physical body. They have forgotten how to let themselves know through total immersion. Everyone talks about rebirth and a new world, but no one's mind understands it. No human mind, that is."

With that thought, the Matriarch Dragon rose to her full height, expanding in front of Fírinne's vision. The great wings lifted her golden body into the heavens amid showers of sparkling stardust. Part of Fírinne rose as a facet of the dragon's heart. She melted into its lines and honeycomb of light. Her ascent left the skies behind as she flowed into alternate ways of being.

This essence she knew with every fiber of her knowing. Fully immersed, she understood that this rebirth can only happen from the inside out. Her inner world opened outward, unfolding like the petals of a rose. Finding home had become an unveiling of the sacred space inside. It was a space she had long known and yearned to inhabit. And, here it was, at long last, carrying her off into the unknown.

Fírinne's shift had hit the fan. She chose to let it blow her away.

September

An Inner Filament Harvest ~ Labradorite

The full moon of September would form at six degrees of Aries. In most tarot decks, the Major Arcana for the number six is the Lovers. In the context of the harvest moon, that archetype could be about reflections of accepting, giving, and receiving love. "If the reflections are internal, as most of these infusions have been, could they show me how I have not been self-loving?"

The question flowed through Fírinne's mind as she rose to greet another day. Sleep had been an elusive gift as the moon waxed toward its perigee. Splashing water on her face, she stretched and prepared to meditate. Her body ached to crawl beneath the covers, but she knew what she had to do. Years of discipline and anticipation of the peace and rejuvenation that always accompanied her meditations helped her to straighten her back and begin.

Fírinne lifted a hand to the thin gold chain about her neck, checking it was still there. The disk it supported, made of gold, had barely any weight. Though tiny, it sang to her throughout her days and nights as she meditated in preparation for the next full moon.

A few days after she donned the necklace, she stepped out of the shower to find it caught in her towel. She placed it on the bathroom counter, noticing that one end had become tangled. "All too easy for these little chains," she grimaced. Then, laughing, she realized, "I must have my dragon lines in a bunch." When she lifted the necklace toward her heart to untangle it, it fell into perfect alignment. The Matriarch Dragon's laughter puffed warm against her neck as she re-clasped the little treasure, marveling at the ease of that adjustment.

Fírinne could feel her meridians dancing. Her awareness resembled a golden puddle. She had not entirely connected how this feeling related to her first awakening. At that time, many years ago, she felt immense peace and no pull toward anything in any way whatsoever. Her current state mirrored that with one gigantic exception. Power. She had never felt so empowered nor such peace.

"Is it time for the next, now?" She asked the Dragon Matriarch. She wondered what could surpass this level of dissolution. Somehow, it was not quite time. So, she sat in the gleaming golden glow, waiting for what was to come.

Fully immersed in the heart of the Matriarch Dragon, it was strange to think of the story continuing. Her mystical training had emphasized grounding. Even though she had experienced walking the world in a state of illumination, she had never felt so absorbed nor immersed in Gaia's magic. Glorious strangeness permeated her awareness, wiping away most of her thoughts. Fírinne had always loved walking meditation, but this was not quite the same.

What magic kept her footfalls from penetrating deep into the earth? What kept her afloat on its surface? She could see and feel the parameters of this life, creating a structural framework for her experience. Though the physical world felt solid, it also felt entirely ephemeral, as though she could sweep it away with a breath. Was part of her afraid to try? Did it seem silly or rude to disdain the gift of this life and this amazing planet?

What magic lay beneath this rural subdivision? What lived under its paved and manicured appearance? Somehow, she knew. She had not lived among this many people for decades. The woods in which she had grown up called to her heart and lifted her spirits above the thought-line of so many. Though trees had been re-planted here, it was not the same. It was not the same. Where was the magic that could feed her open heart?

She chose to walk, though she could barely feel the land through its concrete casings. She walked until she tired and turned for home. Something caught her eye as her footfalls tapped against the pavement. There, precisely in the middle of the manicured square of freshly mown grass that constitutes a front garden, was a young cottontail. S/he could not have been more perfectly centered.

Sitting stone still, it gazed unblinking. "Do rabbits blink?" This one did not. "Oh, you'd best hide," thought Fírinne, feeling her most protective. "There are cats and foxes and other predators about," as if the little one didn't know. The little rabbit remained motionless, intensely still.

Each remained eye-to-eye and heart-to-heart for several more magic minutes. Joy! Heart-surging, overwhelming joy! Respectful of the rabbit's journey, Fírinne shifted her attention and walked toward the front door. When she turned, standing in the open doorway, the rabbit had disappeared. The neighborhood was as it had been. Or was it?

"It is the lunar year of the water rabbit," Fírinne remembered. Rabbit will call our fears and bring them to light, even as the little one is held safe in the Great Mother's arms. From that vantage point, all are securely held, no matter the adventures.

"Let the magic take you. You have become comfortable with giving yourself to the light. Go deeper."

The voice of the dragon echoed through her awareness, unearthing ancient dread. "Why dread the magic? Magic is a word. Words represent concepts and their definitions. All such constructs are temporary at best."

Fírinne realized her early teachings had taken over. She needed to perceive more clearly. Her current awareness rippled, refreshed as with dew. Every cell in her body felt renewed. Her light fibers danced with joy. Was this not magic? What was there to fear?

In a changed world, how could obsolete perceptions help? You have been brought into the essence of what creates worlds. Let yourself be re-formed.

Happy to hear Source's voice again, Fírinne relaxed and listened with all her heart. "Show me," she whispered. That soft request flowed like ripples on the water of her being, like a gentle breeze in whose currents leaves were dancing. She gave herself over. She remembered these tides and how they constantly flow. Suddenly, she recalled a shift in perception she had felt early on in her awakening process. Every nuance of nature had appeared in code. As her lenses of perception shuffled, she could see through their various filters simultaneously. The flowers lining the stairs to her house glowed orange and yellow, their leaves pulsing green with health and vitality. And yet, the inner architecture of each leaf, each bloom, was revealed as strands of living light. Was this happening to her body now? Was she learning to see herself in new ways? It made sense that these lenses of perception had always been present. Yet, somehow, this was new.

"Wait for the moonrise," the dragon told her. "Gladly," she silently sent from within that great heart.

Within the window of the waxing moon, Fírinne positioned herself outdoors. She was comfortably seated on a chaise beneath tall Aspen and Rowan trees as she waited for the next infusion. She gazed at the moon's image and how it pulled her into a newly grounded realm—Fire and Air tempered by the depths of the sea. Its iridescent radiance glowed with tiny ribbons of light. It reminded her of something. What was it? Then she realized Labradorite had stepped up as her ally for this lunation. "Oh, welcome, dear friend!" she gasped as knowledge of this precious ally filled her heart.

The Inuit and the Native American Innu of Labrador claim Labradorite fell from the Aurora Borealis as frozen fire, infusing the northern lights' magic into coastal stone.

In ancient times, the Aurora Borealis rested entombed within these rocks on the shoreline. One day, an Inuit warrior found the shimmering mass and struck the rocks with his spear. The lights exploded into the sky, freeing what we know as the Northern Lights today. However, he couldn't release all of them, which is why we are blessed with the stone of the lights, Labradorite. It is a Stone of Magic, an ally for all who travel and embrace the universe, seeking knowledge and guidance. It is excellent for awakening awareness of inner spirit, intuition, and psychic abilities. It stimulates inner awareness, bringing us closer to our true selves.

Sometimes known as the "temple of the stars," its labradorescence is believed to be of extra-terrestrial origins and enclosed in the mineral to bring the evolved energies from other worlds to the Earth plane. This once-ordinary coastal stone, transformed into something extraordinary, shimmers with a mystical light that veils the waking world from unseen realms.

In Norse mythology, a legend claims that a Mighty Being could stroke these rocks to obtain enough light to travel to the sky. Thus freed, they formed a bridge to the heavens.

In Asian culture, Labradorite was called the "phenomenal gem" to be worn only on specific sacred days. There is also a myth that the lights inside Labradorite are aliens or evolved beings trying to connect to the human world. Fírinne had laughed at that one, though the more time she spent with the stone, the less sure she was of anything about it. Whatever one may or may not believe, the fact remains that the stone is stunning.

Like other dark-colored stones, Labradorite provides a shielding force throughout the aura, strengthening natural energies from within. It protects against the negativity and misfortunes of this world, provides safe exploration into alternate levels of consciousness, and facilitates visionary experiences from the past and the future. It dissipates illusions and strengthens the ability to ground within. It allows one's magical powers to surface.

"Exactly what I need right now," thought Fírinne, as she reviewed the lore of the stone. What fun to be working with an ally she loved so much! What this stone had always spoken to her was that its subtle light lines reflected those of her awareness. How the stone looked to her at any moment was how she looked to herself. Somehow, she was related to these delicate lines of light. These filaments were family, whether encased in matter or lighting up the heavens. It was time to own that relationship.

Keep it close. This essence is part of what you now know yourself to be.

Source's voice rang through the dragon's heart. The structure held Fírinne safe yet beckoned her onward. Luminous threads of labradorescence shimmered and gleamed around her as they undulated within these chambers. Each strand carried an elemental wisdom of its own. Certain strands claimed her attention as they appeared to burn more brightly, then combined with another and another, lighting her way. These she followed, conscious that an expanded awareness and resonance had chosen every pathway.

Each of the dragon's massive heartbeats propelled her further. Body-surfing these pulses, she understood that these pristine elemental energies were those that birthed new worlds. Each heartbeat brought a fresh download and an intense surge of joy.

Firinne's mind momentarily surfaced with the intelligence that waves of higher frequencies had been moving through the world, weaving emerging possibilities and burying what cannot remain. "Yes, of course," she whispered, careful not to disturb the tides of light.

The Great Remembering is bringing the human collective to ancient truths infused with higher octaves of divine light. Any intent to transcend will now take a more individuated form. Like crystals, each will grow according to inner nature rather than that of any collective.

A movement drew her attention to the dragon's great claws. Massive though they were, each grasped delicate strands of luminescence. Pulling these elements together with the utmost finesse, the Matriarch Dragon began to knit the various threads into new designs.

Source spoke through each movement and every fiber of Firinne's absorption.

The stones are of the stars, and the stars are in the stones. These fibers of luminosity are the essence and ground of all beings.

Your mind knows this, as does your heart. Will you allow yourself to know? Will you allow yourself to grow?

At this point, what body awareness Firinne had left shivered in anticipation of a completion involving some sort of untimely death. Still, she faced her fear. These fears must have been deeply buried to have escaped her notice thus far. They had no faces or forms, only an inner quaking that defied logic and reason.

"Breathe with me," toned the dragon's voice. "Your body is not imperiled. It fears its demise. This is only natural when hatching a new reality. Its confusion will pass."

"Hatching?" Fírinne could not help but question, even though she felt the breaking of her reality construct and gratefully absorbed the frequencies of what lay beyond.

Source spoke through the emanations of the dragon's infinite heart.

Remember you have been gestating and are still learning, taking baby steps. Let your essence lead your body to find a way to navigate these new realities. Let Me do that through you. Your mind tends to try to forget the truth of Oneness. It doesn't have to be that way. You don't have to be that way. How might a particle remember its waveform? This is that revelation and that remembrance.

Feel the infinite support of the Oneness, as the One. Are you not forever enmeshed within its filaments of luminosity? Your experience of life has now changed. You cannot go back to old ways of perceiving. Those lenses of perception no longer exist for you. How could a direction like the 'past' possibly exist, from within an integrated whole?

Remember the degree of this lunation, this reflection of your radiant light. In your current understanding, the sign of Aries is about new beginnings within an individuated self. It holds higher octaves of such individuation. At the age of six, the emerging self only begins to learn to navigate. And the sixth degree, the sixth element, is about learning to love.

Every higher frequency, every freshly woven filament, is composed of cosmic love. Like the light on the waters, love shines, illuminating the ripples of each experience. Gaia's consciousness is saturated with every octave of these immersions. The cosmic symphony stands tuned and ready. It has only begun to play.

Golden-lavender light surrounded Fírinne as she opened her eyes. Blue-white luminosity drifted through her body and the space around her. She could see quite clearly what seemed to be a new planet, held together in cohesive consciousness by luminous flows of what could only be love.

"This is Gaia's true nature," whispered the dragon. "This is what my kind, my children, hold dear. We agreed to hold it so, as did you."

Images of a being she had called an 'Earth Angel' in childhood flashed before her eyes. Love poured from this being, encircling the Earth in what looked to be a protective grid of light. Fírinne had always loved the image but never gave it more than a passing thought. Now, merging with the picture, she felt the vast web of love it represented. The essence that encompassed all stars and all such stellar beings flowed through her mind and body in such a way that she almost fainted. Could her body handle this level of intensity? It felt easier to drop into what had been normal to try to maintain some semblance of mental control.

"No," she told herself. "I must ground this through my physical body and into physical life." Struggling a bit, she realized that her eyes were wide open. She sat where she had begun her meditation. Brushing a few fallen leaves from her shoulders, she took slow, careful breaths. Her body felt stiff and chilled. She ached for her shawl and a cup of tea. But that could wait.

Everything around her looked brighter and more clearly defined. The Autumn leaves of sheltering Aspens glowed golden. Orange Rowan berries shone like the sun. She stirred on her chaise. As she did so, her movement caused a fluttering and scattering among the squirrels and birds that filled the trees around her. Each being beamed with its own unique radiance. She could not help but smile. "What an incredible world. And what is yet to be?"

Not yet ready to stand, Fírinne took a deep, quavering breath and gazed at the garden around her. A single cottontail sat, planted on the grass a few feet in front of her. An embodiment of stillness, patience, and peace, the sight of the little one swelled her already bursting heart. Glowing threads of light flowed between her body, the rabbit, and the entire garden. With that vision, she remembered. "The whole world lives within the cosmic heart of home."

She laughed, startling her visitor. A water rabbit year indeed, she thought, as the cottontail's little white flag disappeared into the verge. "May we all become so easily absorbed."

In the days and weeks that followed, Fírinne saw mystical lines of light everywhere she looked. Observing the mystical nature of her surroundings became second nature. The lines became increasingly present, whether her eyes were open or closed. And then, everything changed again.

October

The Hunter's Moon ~ Banding Together ~ Fluorite

Fírinne's perspective had exploded. Labradorite helped her to ground what made no sense to her sensory array.

"My field is like the Labradorite, laced with the essence of each jewel of transformation," Fírinne whispered. Lines of luminosity formed what looked like cracks in her field. Each fracture created an opening with specific and unique qualities. Each facet between the cracks held a particular worldview, defined by color and frequency. Realization moved through her field, helping to shape the vision. "The edges of each facet of fractured field form planes of reality. I am that field. Source is the warp, the infinite strings of a divine harp. New jewel tones provide the weft for a new way."

Source's transmission flowed through Fírinne's thoughts with pristine clarity, blurring all lines of separation. The knowledge that she walked a newly-evolving waking dream was almost too much. Almost. She had never been so grateful for her early training. "Hold steady. Stay the course. This may be a deeper integration than I have ever experienced. Let's wait and see." Her physical body was in a constant state of exhaustion, though her inner awareness radiated joy.

Points of light grew into bubbles coming to the surface of an ever-shifting reality. The bubbles penetrated bands of perception as though no boundaries existed. Almost invisible veils glowed white enough to be clearly seen, wafting in transparent wisps over glimpses of seas of cosmic turbulence. What seemed to be a reality construct of infinite color and light created a buffer between Fírinne and All That Is. Her vision showed her fractures in every direction. Delicate lines of exquisite geometric patterns laced the world through and around her. When closely observed, each vanished into the whole. "Waveforms only," she supposed. "This, too, shall pass" was how she had been taught to deal with visual phenomena. "Pay attention to what lies beneath, what is being revealed."

She had been taught all about projection and how perception varies according to the filters anyone carries. Looking at the fractured lines around her, she began to wonder. "Will everyone see differently? Is all of life breaking apart?"

Only the old life, the old worlds you have lived within.

She used to wonder what people saw when they looked at her. Memories of the girl she had been surfaced within and behind her field's visual splits and cracks. None of what she was seeing made sense. Then, she realized she had become accustomed to projecting the realities of her teachers around her like weird factory-setting defaults. She felt and knew the truth that none of these default settings were truly her own. She had taken the worldviews of her mentors for granted, even when the core of her disagreed.

Those default settings seemed like such old, dealt-with, and discarded information. The energy stored in such patterns had long ago been repurposed. Fírinne had not bought into most of those definitions for ages. And yet, she saw where her field still operated as though it belonged to others. Her initial dismantling process began more than half a lifetime ago. She had worked through filter after filter, wave after wave of those versions of reality, re-absorbing their energies into her core. "Nothing teaches us more quickly than life's reflections," she mused.

Those early alterations were obvious. These were far more subtle. Yesterday's reflections seemed to be a mosaic of bits of projected images for 'sky,' not the whole of it but sectioned fractals, or 'tree,' wherein every leaf stood out clearly and distinctly, and yet, the tree or trees were sectioned by fine lines of light, like the threads of a rutilated quartz crystal, representing a new kind of structure with as yet unexamined qualities. She had never before perceived her learning bubble in this way.

She sat in the garden in that lovely golden late afternoon light that always heralds Autumn. Looking up at the sky, she could see each section of her fractured reality clearly defined. She raised her hand and folded one piece of trees-and-sky toward her as though the reality construct was origami. "Would there be star fields behind it? Would her action make a difference?"

But, no. There was only more sunlit sky. She made a few more folds, just for fun, then pushed them back into their original places, unsure if disturbing them was appropriate. The glowing lines shone brightly, but Fírinne had yet to understand what she was seeing. The movements to fold various corners had been instinctual, but still, she hesitated, feeling that non-interference was likely the best course.

"The full moon forms tomorrow," she realized. "The sooner, the better! This perceptual opening is fantastic, but I have no idea how it needs to ground."

The lines of light are the lines of the world weaving and re-weaving.

An early evening chill embraced the garden. And so Fírinne rose from her seat beneath the trees and shuffled through drifts of crackling leaves toward the door. The feel of the leaves and the bracing quality of light and air told her the Hunter's Moon window had begun. She could hardly wait until tomorrow.

The Hunter's Moon was dear to Fírinne's heart. In the woods, one might see deer, turkeys, and bears preparing for winter. And, every Hunter's Moon was sacred to the Goddess Archetype of Diana. Her silver bow, unerring in its accuracy, always aims at truth. The thinning of the veils during the Samhain window spoke to this. Fírinne always felt herself launched like one of Diana's arrows into a more authentic path, into something more. She wondered how she could be more of herself, how this Hunter's Moon might be more significant than any other.

This Hunter's Moon highlights what each person searches for and where they feel hunted. It asks how anyone can feel safe. Given the world as it was, some answers might not be what anyone would want to hear. "I want to hear," thought Fírinne. "I am open to new knowing."

Early the following morning, she woke from a dream. She had been in an office of some kind, working with a computer system that penetrated realities. The lens she looked through was only wide enough for her vision and no one else's. Its screen had been installed in an odd place, hidden beneath the desktop, where it was largely inaccessible. A large screen on the desktop showed multiple realities. In the small screen capsule reality, she watched as the edges of the tiny view-screen folded into a two-dimensional pentagonal shape, which then rendered into a multi-dimensional starseed Merkaba with twelve points. Each point had five faces, lit up like prisms. And, from the center of that form, her own eyes peered back at her. "Oh!" The recognition was immediate.

The realization of unity within filtered realities came without words or conceptual knowledge. She woke from the dream with the crystalline structure gleaming around her. Meditation yielded fresh perspectives but few words. "Probably just as well," she thought. "When our old images shatter, we don't need interim falsities to replace them."

Fírinne began to meditate to receive the full moon download indoors, as the day had turned cold. Still, her chair rested beneath the spreading boughs of a mature Maple whose leaves had not entirely fallen. Despite the roof overhead, she felt held within and protected by the green world. She nestled into her chair and surrendered into Oneness.

When Fírinne's vision opened, light bubbles burst through what looked like crystal lenses striped with pure luminescent color. Clear, greenish blue, and purple, with occasional flashes of rose, the bands of color reflected bandwidths of frequency, creating multi-colored gems of creative energy. As each bubble burst through the colored bands, it took on a striped or multi-colored appearance, then softened into what looked like a gelatinous, formless form, infusing the planet and her body. Some globules rested within a form for a few moments only, some infused into existing structures, and some moved on.

Fluorite, the genius stone, had stepped up as an ally for the Hunter's Moon. According to mineral mythology, its presence heralded a time of preservation, transition, divination, and balance. She realized that Fluorite provided bands of perception for each lunar integration.

"Rainbow Fluorite is a crystal of soul purpose and dharma. This gem assists me in living with grace and in truth to the highest call and purpose of my life."

With that realization, bands of color and frequency began to ripple through the world and her body. Her field became fluid like the sea, each wave carrying multiple currents, multiple ripples of colored light. She watched as these swells of attention picked up elements from each lunation, melding them into a unified whole.

Pearlescent completions moved her into enfoldment in the arms of the Great Mother. Allies and insights came from her Celtic memories and the Great Mother's cycle of life. A misted quartz-like prism opened into a glimpse of her initial vision of the Pearl. That journey seemed long ago and far away. She saw now that it had been an initiation into re-entry through the womb of the Great Mother. What joy! The moonlight she had imbibed through her cupped palms illumined her spirit companions, the light and the coalescing birth waters.

She began to see from within the womb of life. Wispy lines of the world's energies widened into ribbons of light. A ribbon of sapphire blue spread itself across her face, covering both her physical eyes and her third eye. As she blinked through the Sapphire prism, galactic bands of perception opened to her. Stars and galaxies emerged into view. She was one with the deep infinity of space, held within the Mother's orb of light. And she could see! "This Sun is a yellow star," she remembered. "It masks layers of perception by making the yellow spectrum stronger. That must have something to do with how humans view chakras and dimensions."

Keep looking. You will see.

Aquamarine energies infused her being. Her whole body glowed with translucent, healing bluish-green. Deep sapphire tones lightened into softer hues. She soared high, the eagle's perspective showing how these energetic infusions melted into Gaia from the depths of the Cosmic womb. Afloat in their support, she basked in rejuvenation.

"Gaia is pregnant with a new version of herself." The Matriarch Dragon's voice growled softly. "Each infusion informs the birth waters. Let yourself be carried."

The essence of Pounamu grounded her field, showing her the flow of its journey as a particle through currents of the world's ley lines. From the peaks to the seas, it tumbled, hardened, broke apart, and tumbled once more as a flow of divinity revered and honored. So had her journey formed and shattered and re-shaped her being.

Then Moonstone appeared, infused through the Celtic lands, steeped in Gaia's magic. Fírinne recalled the upsurge of frequencies from the Solstice in June and how it sluiced away old stories and lives and kindled new loves. New choices had led her here, where whispers of light wove new realities. These feelings were strange yet intimately and intensely familiar.

Ruby essence rose through her heart, first in its faceted, blood-red aspect, then softening into a deep, rosy glow. "Strength," it whispered. "Courage. Remember your dragon self. Remember the heart of the stag."

Fire Quartz, its veins of hematite radiating physical strength, rose up her spine to support this transformation. An engine-like pillar of fire ignited every vertebra. Rising Kundalini had never felt like this before! Its passage shifted bone marrow and cartilage and re-calibrated each nerve root.

Amber flowed through her veins as though she was a tree. Its distilled essence liquified until it ran through her like the sap it once had been. Fully grounding her into Gaia, it moved further, merging with the magmatic elementals deep beneath the Earth's crust. Reaching the stellar heart of the planet, this melding of mineral and green world surged upward once more, rising with the tide of emergence.

Heart feels everything. Fírinne's held all the world. In the kernel of a world gone weird, amid wild acting out, something marvelous was forming. Yet all of this was implicit, inherent, and inward, invisible to outer eyes.

These strands of luminosity are the seeds that have been through the fire to attain what is true and lasting.

The concepts made no sense to her mind, but the Great Mother's transmission flowed through Fírinne's heart like waves. From there, she understood them all.

Amethyst lines of light threaded through her body like arteries and veins, rearranging her physiology along new meridians of consciousness. Pure, unclouded perception showed her the depths of this transformation that altered worlds. And then, she was back inside a Labradorite egg, suspended amid nascent lacings of creative force.

The dark background of the stone was a perfect canvas for the delicate dance of light she had witnessed. And so, she rested in its depths as though she lay on the sea floor, watching sunlight at play. What had been fine, pristine flows widened into a more cohesive spectral array. Each of the jewels' contributing energies had integrated to some degree. And Fluorite provided bands of perception for each integration.

"What might come next?" she thought, thoroughly immersed in wonder.

The Matriarch Dragon drew Fírinne's vision to the Himalayas. "At last," her Spirit breathed. "All my life, I have looked for this."

"Is this my feeling of home or yours?" she asked, half expecting the dragon to laugh at her presumption.

"Why does it have to be one or the other?" the dragon's voice softened as it faded away.

The great mountain ranges of Nepal and Tibet filled Fírinne's heart. Their majesty cleansed her field as she breathed great gulps of frigid air. Power spot after power spot radiated its unique light, forming a node in the vast network of rarified frequencies she floated within. Fractal after fractal of vision flowed through the kaleidoscope she had become. Were these reflections those of memory, or what now needed to be let go?

Open your eyes! The command came directly from Source.

Bare branches stretched across Fírinne's visual field. She stood, shifting her perspective to the whole tree outside her window. On the street side, its branches were bare and rattling a bit. On the side above the roof and her chair, sheltering leaves of many colors stirred in a sunlit breeze. It reminded her of sacred artwork depicting the seam between Autumn and Winter, one-half of the tree's branches filled with leaves, the other bare and dusted with snow. "What generous support!" she and the tree voiced, linked essence to essence, curled together in the armchair of silence.

The deep, nurturing stillness of the Himalayas cradled her. Rishi after Rishi welcomed the new emergence. Temple after temple, stupa after stupa reverberated, rang, with new light. "Welcome, oh welcome," sang the mountains on the roof of the world, as integrating frequencies flooded their existence. And as they sang, each jewel contributed its harmonics. A new symphony had begun.

Celestite emerged through the lens of the heights. Its delicate grace shone through the Himalayas, illuminating them from the inside out.

November

The Beaver Moon ~ Beginning to Build ~ Celestite

Awed by the emergence of a new ally, Fírinne sat with a piece of Celestite in her cupped hands. Its translucent sky-blue glow mirrored her inner landscape. She knew her mind was resisting, ever so slightly, the onslaught of celestial information flowing to and through her. She hoped the mineral ally would help her to ground and receive. Fírinne knew that the full moon of November would fall at 4 degrees 51 minutes of Gemini. This position would put the alignment between the vibrations of four and five. The numerology felt significant as part of a more remarkable shift happening on the planet, so Fírinne revised some of what she had learned about these symbols.

The Sabian symbol for four, per Dane Rudhyar, read, "...beneath the surface we long for something we know is lost or forgotten, something more real, closer to Nature." Given this year's infusions, that felt relevant.

She remembered that four is a grounding structure, marking a dimension of life, potentially taking thought beyond established limits and collective opinions.

In the Major Arcana, four is the Emperor card. It denotes external authority and a need to step into power without fear. Depending on the position in a reading, The Emperor can also represent someone else taking control away from you or blocking you from embodying power. The Tarot depicts this as a male card, which can indicate tethers to patriarchal authority.

"Enough of those," Fírinne sighed. "And five is always about how our lives hold power." The 5th card in the tarot is the Hierophant, who allegedly provides spiritual knowledge and guidance. Also a traditionally male card, the switch from Emperor to Hierophant, four to five, indicates a shift from outer to inner authority. It shows that the querent seeks advice in spiritual matters or guidance from a teacher or Guru figure.

"That was certainly an old-cycle interpretation," thought Fírinne as she closed her books and prepared to meditate. "If these lunations have shown me anything, it is that Source's true light wells from within everything." She knew her upcoming journey would change all definitions of everything, and she felt ready. The Himalayas had been calling her ever since the most recent new moon. She had no idea why but knew she must respond with everything she was. These last two infusions would be critical to her metamorphosis.

The flight to Kathmandu took it out of her. Taking the time to acclimate to higher altitude was a wise and necessary pause. She knew, from experience, that it was best to travel slowly here, where timelessness governs the flow of life. Like the savanna of South Africa, where the herds are constantly on the move, the stillness of the mountains amplified every movement. Pilgrims and trekkers flowed along well-established trails. Flocks and herds followed their ancestral migratory patterns. The whole world seemed to move, supported by an uplift of stillness.

Two days into the mountains from Kathmandu, Fírinne felt comfortably settled into the meditative energy of the small stone house built near a squat stone temple. Bright blue paint framed each window. Rolled books lined an entire wall in diamond-shaped cubbyholes. Brightly colored prayer flags flew from the roof at each peak and corner, while those particular to the caretakers adorned a dedicated pole. She could almost hear the prayers being lifted into the ethers by the ever-present wind.

Spare though the accommodations were, Fírinne was satisfied. Her sleeping alcove was enough. This journey was a mystical adventure, not a vacation. She touched the cabochon of Celestite carefully tucked between the woolen layers beneath her jacket, ensuring once more that it had not become dislodged during the trek. Satisfied that her traveling companion lay warm against her breastbone, she reviewed the hike.

It had been quite the climb, aided by experienced guides and a few domesticated yaks. The local inhabitants were invariably kind and considerate, an integral part of the culture she had come to immerse within. Each lived a life so profoundly spiritual that the peace of the Himalayas flowed through its day-to-day life unimpeded.

The trail wound upward through a fragrant forest and its shifting, enchanted light. Glimpses of snowy peaks through gaps in the branches teased her senses while the heat from the brilliant morning sun helped her forget her aching muscles.

Loosely constructed wooden bridges lashed together with whatever was available, lined with the rippling pastels of fading prayer flags, made paths across waters whose rushing sounds could still be heard beneath their cloak of ice.

Guides and yaks moved on after sharing a meal at her destination, leaving Fírinne ensconced in the temple's pool of cultivated silence. Sitting and sipping tea, she thought, "I'm unsure I would have noticed if my pack had disappeared with the animals. My burdens certainly have." And then the moon rose behind the peaks. "Full tomorrow," she said to no one in particular. "Yes," the smiling face of one of the caretakers replied, echoing her joy.

She woke early to the sounds and smells of the waking temple. Incense smoke filled the air, as did the trail of steam following the ancient woman who brought her a fresh cup of tea. Deep wrinkles wreathed a broad smile as the woman handed over the steaming cup. Her long, steely-soft braid whispered against her jacket as she silently turned and left, a wooden mala flowing, bead by bead, through one gnarled hand.

Sipping her cup of butter tea, Fírinne gazed at Kailas in the distance. Its holy peak is so sacred it is banned from climbers, even by the Chinese government. Its snow-capped summit gleamed white in the morning sun, reflecting light in all directions. The source of four rivers, the Indus, Sutlej, Brahmaputra, and Karnali, each flowing in a cardinal direction, its peak towered above the surrounding mountains, even in this place, protected on all sides by walls of rock and ice.

"Thank you for the simple enjoyment of my simple life," Fírinne whispered. Tea sipped to the accompanying hum of morning prayers—the opportunity to receive this latest infusion in a place primed to embody its blessings. Concealed within the embrace of the mountains, she embraced the solitude and clarity of the moment and knew she was where she needed to be.

Above the clouds lives the perspective of Oneness. Within view of some of the holiest mountains in the world, Fírinne was ready to perceive in new ways. Swallowing the remainder of her tea, she sank into meditation.

The transmission from this lunation surrounded and embraced her entire body, making her essence indistinguishable from that of the mountain. Its voice shook her to the roots of everything she was. She could feel the infinite depths of stone connected with the stars. Spread out before her vision, the whole world seemed to be restructuring behind the scenes. And what scenes! Stars blazed with pristine clarity, close enough to be plucked. Their cold luminosity formed a perfect backdrop for the rising moon, whose silvery glow bathed the surrounding walls of ice.

Emerging from her vision, she felt the glimmer of daylight resonating gently through the Celestine stone which nestled against her heart. At night, its essence was that of starlight. With the moon's rise, she could feel its light, too, glowing softly against her skin. "Starlight and reflected sunlight," she smiled to herself. "How precious."

Fírinne considered this special ally and how it had become part of her journey. A very delicate mineral, Celestite lends itself more to tumbling than cutting and faceting because it breaks so easily. It doesn't like the pressure that dictates that it should conform to someone else's idea of what a jewel should look like.

In the mystical traditions, Celestite is honored for its angelic radiance and as a receptacle for divine consciousness. It is worn to assist with spiritual courage and transcendence. But, from Fírinne's point of view, one of the most amazing things about Celestite is that it begins its life in collaboration with tiny protozoan creatures called Acantharea. These single-celled creatures bond with the element strontium and biomineralize, much like our cells, as they change carbon content to silica.

These beings then shift and create an incredible crystal that radiates soft, angelic, divine energy. They are the only creatures discovered so far that create crystal-fibrous skeletons that make them look like stars.

"A single-cell creature that looks like a star," mused Fírinne. And what a perfect ally for choosing based on new vistas of sight, as it shows up for a lunation blowing away all third-eye and physical vision and all ideations of the mind. Now, that is a catalyst for true presence. True. Mindful. Meditative. Reverent. Presence. A mineral being that does not fossilize, it crystallizes. "If I think about what's happening to my body right now, what a perfect ally!"

The resonance of Celestite had so merged with that of the mountain that Fírinne initially had trouble discerning it. She watched and listened as it infused the world's high places. She felt it within the atmosphere, the waters, the earth, the ridges, peaks, and their interconnecting valleys. With moonrise, the resonance began to move. It sang through new filaments of light, the way stellar light used to move through the pyramids of the old world.

This elemental form of starlight was precisely aligned with all pyramids and created an energy grid throughout the planet, Fírinne remembered. Now, she watched as a higher octave surge flowed through the natural world. It activated a higher network of light within all Earth centers and all embodied physical centers. She wondered if the local yaks felt the change and giggled at the thought of those stolid creatures vibrating with the stars.

"Mystics aspire to these vibrations," she thought. "And these lines of light show up as a support through the land humans walk upon and the air they breathe. This infusion is the beginning of a new foundational way of life.

The shift transcends all old ideas about what empowerment is.

Here is the essence of nurturing empowerment. How can power nurture this world? The dragons know. Their electromagnetic currents have long nourished the ley lines of this planet. Dragon energy is so strong here. Does it amplify cellular starlight in all creatures?"

The moon's reflection provided silvery-white illumination. Creature allies had presented themselves for each full moon. Whose essence was present now? And would dragon lines lace through all beings?

Fírinne recalled that in the indigenous traditions of the Northernmost Americas, the full moon of November is sometimes called the Beaver Moon. Beaver is a builder, an embodiment of productivity and open options. It embodies persistence and the cunning use of available resources. Beaver utilizes the dynamics of teamwork to accomplish anything, even constructing shelter across moving currents.

"The nature of every shelter is changing and morphing, and so very malleable at this time. How is it possible to live with this energy that wants to build, construct, and do this holistically?"

An image of a platypus formed in Fírinne's vision. "Odd," she thought. "A creature from the other end of the world." Information flowed through her vision in answer to her question. Platypuses do things differently than beavers do. They hide their dens. They use the protective energy of the Earth to nest. Newborns emerge from the egg and are nurtured for one day only. Then they go off and learn how to live. Platypuses use the thousands of mechanoreceptors and electroreceptors in their unique bills to detect movements and subtle electric fields produced by their environment and prey. They live by an awareness of subtle energies.

Humans are very much like the platypus right now. The most conscious are magical beings that seem like they can't exist here. This lunation initiates new flavors and textures of life, better internally experienced than mentally designed.

Experience the flow of the water. Experience, as the platypus does, what nourishment is available. Experience as the beaver does. "Here's what I've built. Here's my structure. Here's how I protect everything." This year's infusions of celestial energy are the melt that washes it all away. It is like building the perfect sandcastle. And then the wave wipes it out. Or the perfect sand painting, whose purpose is to be destroyed to illustrate impermanence.

The world is awash in impermanence. This flooding is needed to open hearts to open understanding. For those who are here to ground this, simply by being, nothing needs to be done. Be the clear light. Wherever you are right now, let it flow through you. Let the magic of what is happening light you up. Let it blow all ideas of you away. Like those little single-celled organisms that become crystals, your cells are shifting.

Source's voice was welcome in the midst of all that swirled around and through Fírinne's consciousness. Thoroughly at peace, she rested in Silence as the flood of transformation washed through her.

You have lived in a bubble, trying to hold it together with your will. Exhausting, is it not? Let your bubble disappear rather than fall apart. That is where fear tries to take you. Let it all disappear and move into an authentic, abundant, prosperous sovereignty that has nothing to do with having it your way or with any old definition of power.

Fírinne had spent the past weeks watching the cells of her body morph. She wondered if this was similar to what Celestite must feel as it morphs from the inside out into crystalline form. Her cellular transformation began with the October full moon and now seemed to be integrating. How was her shift similar to that of the stone?

Feel the dragon that has swallowed you. You now exist within her heart and body. You have merged with the electromagnetic flows that are magic in this world. Let them express themselves through you, even in unfamiliar ways.

Each cell in your body is going through this process. Let your inner perceptions rise and dissolve as you look for new wonders. Oh, look, there's a platypus! A unicorn! In these parts? A dragon. Something extraordinary is building a life through you. Those embodied on this planet are becoming the infusion to participate in the joy of new creation.

Galactic birth waters are moving through the heights. It begins here, in the Himalayas, the Andes, the Rockies, and the Alps of every location. Where will it go after that? The dragons know. These infinitely intelligent, loving electromagnetic currents know. They are the infusions moving through less populated, less developed areas. It is a practical infusion in that way and forward-looking. Forward-drawn like that Sagittarian arrow, and pointing through the pillars of Gemini and into infinite choice. What if either/or was irrelevant?

Earlier that morning, Fírinne had dreamed. She was outdoors, on a mountainside in summer, gathering herbs for new planting. She remembered seeking Echinacea. She found a patch and asked for the right stem, the one which wanted to come with her and be part of a new garden. She tugged at it slightly and it came easily out of the ground. She tucked it into her basket. And then she heard, "Gather four more." The energy moved from four to five. Each herb that volunteered to come with her would be lovingly, tenderly put into the ground in a special place. Each planting would be intended with so much light and so much joy. The green world was so very present and wanted to participate. Each plant appreciated being asked and honored.

Does this one want to be part of a new garden? Not that the others will be left behind. Gaia knows how to take care of her own. But there's something extraordinary being seeded. In the dream, what showed up were seedlings, not the dormant seeds of winter. These sprouts held the beginnings of new life.

"What will be nourished and nurtured? What will grow? What will be fed with intent?" Questions fired through Fírinne's heart as she drifted out of meditation.

The answers move through you even now. The clear light reshapes every moment. Let the obsolete patterns finally meet their demise. Let the light matter more than anything else. What matters manifests. The natural world. The beavers and the platypuses and the Celestite and the mountains and the valleys and the water. Huge tides, this day. Ride them well.

Fírinne's door hangings swung open at the perfect moment, admitting the ancient caretaker, holding a fresh cup of tea. Etched into the sides of the cup was a white dragon. The caretaker pointed at the ferocious-looking creature, then at Fírinne, sending both women into gales of laughter.

The Tibetans have a saying, "Recognition is liberation."

December

The Cold Moon ~ Reset ~ Selenite

Returning from the Himalayas felt timeless. Fírinne felt out of body, time, and form. Though she physically traveled from one part of the world to another, one mountain range to another, it felt like she was standing still.

Somehow, she went through the motions, supported by the electromagnetic lacings of Gaia's ley lines and emerging energy grid. She could feel those currents physically in ways she never had before. The upcoming Solstice waves removed the old grids, inside and out.

She made her sunrise cup of tea, fully aware that her consciousness now extended beyond the boundaries of the Sun. Her smile cherished the day star and its life-giving light. As she waited for the tea kettle's plume of steam, she pondered the quality of this light.

"Sunlight waxes in the sky, and the light of the other stars fades. Everything is a question of proximity and influence, especially wild card energy, where anything can happen. When a celestial body, like a planet or a moon, appears outside the Sun's north-south path along the ecliptic, galactic energy surges into the solar system, bringing trickster energy, and circumstances are ripe for change. So am I," she thought, "So am I."

The final lunation, the mystical 13th moon, would form out of bounds at 4.58 degrees of the zodiac sign of Cancer. Out of bounds, she mused, outside of the box. Something was about to happen.

The lunar alignment shifts to inner authority, nourishment, and nurturing. It presents fresh forms and new archetypes to explore. In Fírinne's vision, these forms flowed fluidly in unrecognizable shapes. How would they coalesce into something cohesive? How would they be nurtured?

The Continental Divide rippled, its rivers roaring, as its snow-capped dragon's back arched and stretched. Long dormant, the dragon line purred as it awakened. Fírinne felt the humming deep in her bones.

The new energies require new ways to ground, a new responsibility for integration, and an openness to receive this quickening.

Fírinne welcomed the assistance of Source's voice within her. She had seen that the return of the Cancerian energies was a homecoming. Unity surged through the mountain ranges, mirrored in her spinal column. The feeling was entirely strange and completely supportive. When she formed the thought, "The mountains have my back," the dragon line burst out laughing.

Do ley lines laugh? She supposed so, as the essence of this particular dragon and the Matriarch Dragon finally surfaced locally. The dragon energy of the Continental Divide showed herself as a deep copper-brown, phasing through the greens and browns Fírinne knew as the hues of Earth and Wood elements.

"You think my essence is fixed?" sang the dragon. "Is yours?"

The dragons' voices continued. "How you move, eat, drink, think, or do anything is a powerful doorway to examining how you nourish yourself. Ask yourself what you truly require. Let yourself be still enough to hear the answer. It is time to bring what nurtures you into your field. Once you have accomplished this, those definitions and concepts will be free to morph into a new reality experience."

"Thank you," Fírinne whispered as she watched the Rockies ripple north into Canada and south through the Andes. The heart of this morphing was all around her. It felt like a tremendous seismic event with no discernible epicenter. Her whole world shook and trembled. She felt it in every cell. Meanwhile, the snowy crest of the Continental Divide rested peacefully outside her window.

The Matriarch Dragon came more and more to the fore of Fírinne's meditations as the full moon approached. With one mighty swipe, she flung Fírinne's research on the properties of the so-called Cold Moon into a spiral vortex that spun out from the dragon's heart into the cosmos.

"All things must change. This is what happens." Dragon purrs and angelic choirs provided the lift for this phasing. Leaps and surges of multi-dimensional images flashed through Fírinne's vision as she contemplated the Solstice, the upcoming Full Moon, and the new calendar year ahead.

She had read that the Cold Moon prompts spiritual themes of rest, renewal, and the acknowledgment of shadow whose patterns are being released. Lines of light swirled through this introspective cauldron advocating self-care, conscious living, and the compassionate exploration of hidden aspects of all of life. This moon drew her in as its light became brighter in the night sky. Other names for the full moon closest to the December Solstice are the long night moon, or long day moon, in the southern hemisphere, or the oak moon, she remembered.

The oak tree had always been a favorite. It holds a complete ecosystem within its being. Its roots intertwine with the root systems of the planet; its branches lift into the heavens. Oak represents the World Tree in the Celtic lands. Mycelium fibers and various insect colonies weave their realities within its bark. Acorns are its fruit and seeds, holding renewal and immortality in a small capped package. Oak also stands for the seasonal shift from the cold months into summer.

Embrace the stillness and free hidden emotions. Let the Cold Moon guide you through this opening of celestial wisdom and renewal. Look at what lies beneath any seemingly cold, frozen, or static surface. The gold you have become lies ready to be discovered.

That made a kind of sense to Fírinne. She had felt an internal golden quality since her return from the Himalayas that she could not have put into words until now. She wondered what the coming lunation would reflect.

The Solstice surge dissolved leftover bits of her identities and their support systems. Amid this divine chaos, a new orb of infusion waxed with the moon. Its amorphous essence glowed with sparkling clues to what was happening. Was there a gem ally stepping up to assist?

"Selenite," she heard. As that thought formed, a piece of Selenite on her bookshelf grabbed her attention. "Was it glowing? Or was she finally aligned enough with its essence so she could hear its voice?"

She had seen Selenite used as an essential tool in spiritual practices due to its ability to hold and resonate with higher vibrational energies. Were these latest infusions using it as a conduit?

"It is no wonder that Selenite is named for Selene, Goddess of the Moon," she thought. "The mineral's resonance promotes peace, calm, mental clarity, and well-being. It is known for rejuvenating and aligning the spinal column with divine feminine energy and flexibility and is often used to purify, cleanse, and align energy multi-dimensionally. If the essence of this year's progression of thirteen jewels was transformation, it made sense that the grounding conduit would be one that could handle what was to come."

"So can I," Fírinne's body chimed in. "I am ready." It was time to move fully into meditation and receive.

In meditation, Fírinne watched as leftover remnants of old patterns shed their energetic content, and Selenite fibers moved in, replacing those old connections in the same way as a building is re-wired. This was not only a re-wiring, though. The energy trapped in old patterns was repurposed, integrating with her essence to hold more light.

The crystalline cellular structure provided by Celestite bonded with these fibers, creating an entirely new architecture in her body and the world. No wonder her physical body felt odd. It wanted to curl in on itself like a fetus and begged for rest. She could feel old habits of behavior wishing to move into trauma response and pulses of more powerful electromagnetic current replacing those obsolete reactions. She sensed the cellular reset and her physical systems' response to the energetic demand for rejuvenation. "It is only too much for my mind," she gasped, asking her body to release through conscious breathing. "Remember what you learned about biophotonics. The body is also light. Each conscious breath draws in peace and grace-infused power."

A third breath brought her the stillness she craved. The velocity of her inward spiral blurred her attention, dropping her into the Stillpoint, the Source that is the Infinite field.

An entirely new operating system was instantiated at the recent

Solstice, and this lunation is shining a reflective light on the nurturing and sustaining qualities of a new way of being. It is about living more consciously from this stillness. Mortality of the physical body is an issue, and, for many, the eternality, the invincibility of Spirit, is coming to the fore.

This frequency infusion is an enlivening, an empowerment of functional freedom as flow.

It instantiates a different kind of foundation as functional flow takes hold. Feel how this lunation, the orb of reflected light, transports you into an entirely new field of perception. All timelines, tracks, and trajectories alter according to how they are perceived.

This coming year of 2024 will be all about alterations in perception. It certainly will be challenging for many. You who see the light streams and the star streams and in and between the worlds will experience moments of "...did not see that coming," and then laugh because you have become the knowledge that this particular seeing was not needed.

Fírinne felt her body shift into a more comfortable alignment as she continued to be absorbed in vision and transmission. Wary of leaving her body, she wiggled her toes, giggling as light waves rippled through her inner and outer realities. This was fun! As her thoughts dissolved, she felt ecstatically blissful, like being immersed in liquid light. Her body felt supported in every cell, even as each morphed completely.

This lunation completes a circuit of inner knowledge about nurturing. The cycle of 13 moons begins and ends in the sign of Cancer, which holds energetic architecture for nourishing and nurturing and embodying those qualities more than any imagined doings. The archetype bears a vibrational imprint and a physical template for nurturing and nourishing embodiment. These woven threads of light have come full circle.

Sense the trinary golden threads that appeared in your initial vision. You can think of three dragons intertwined and swimming through the year, then grabbing one another by the front claws, paws, or jaws, physically and vibrationally holding completion in their circle.

You are those flows. You are those dragon lines. The circuits of your energy bundle, your configuration, contain this gift. You call this day Boxing Day. The unboxing of what resides within you is not the opening and unwrapping of a particular gift; it is the dissolution of the unyielding formats, the fixed templates, and the rigid walls of what blinds you to being present.

Fírinne watched as filter after filter fell away. The mirror ball turned inward as what she knew as her current reality construct cracked, shattered, and dropped away. She almost laughed out loud as she saw through many iterations of her illusions of truth. Source, in the form of an immense wave, lifted her into a functional flow of guidance.

Live from and as this flow.

With that, Fírinne knew, as the wave knows, the breadth and depth of every droplet within her embrace. Living in complete alignment meant living each moment sourced by, impulsed by, every movement orchestrated by an intent so powerful nothing could deter it from its course.

"The Invincible Force!" Fírinne had learned about the Shakti, the Shekinah, and Divine Feminine Grace in her studies and was familiar with many archetypal forms of this energy. She had encountered, worked with, and committed herself to these flows of Sacred Essence. She felt her commitment, with gratitude, aligned in her very core. "As that essence," dragon voices corrected. "Not separate, but as Presence Herself."

You function as a bubble of perception, an orb of energy, and within ripples, currents, and rivers. One of the shifts in perception this lunation brings is freeing the particle from its self-defining limitations. You tend to perceive yourself as particular rivulets or currents or waves of light, as though you were outside of them. That is not the most functional perception for this time. Be absorbed within the Great Mother's tides. There are parts of you that are rivulets, currents, and waves. You are becoming tides.

Tides of light. Tides of love. Waves of supportive sustainability that must move through your body as the fractals of Gaia that they are, and then radiate and join, like the architecture of the flower of life. Conjoining sets of ripples will sustain this new functionality.

This lunation's perceptual shift is that you begin to see, feel, and know your energetic configuration for what it is as a fractal of the Great Wave. Ebb and flow are a shoreline's perspective. The wave perceives only the dance. You are realizing a more unconditional embodiment of cosmic flow.

You must now stand firm in whatever way is most supportive for you. Let the higher vibrations move through you. They know what to do. You know when you are called. You always know. Your deepest part knows how, to what, and by what. This lunation dissolves and removes the denials from their imagined containers. Let your mind's descriptors and concepts release with the wave. Let these exquisite prisms of light move through you.

Feel your energies being gathered into this lunation, into what is happening, to this new platform, to this new operating system that was instantiated at the Solstice. It gathers you up like a mother lion grabs a cub, cradling and supporting you. This is a mature, sustaining, nurturing expression of love. Maturation into your divinity is expanding. This expansion requires strength, patience, and surrender.

The structures you feel in your body have been called the diamond body. You recognize the signature of profound star field energy; feeling yourself held, supported, enfolded, and embraced by all you require. This year, these thirteen lunations have been an infusion of the powers that create this new platform, world, and paradigm. And it was all preparation for what is to come.

You are that which you need the most. So, let yourself open, allow, and receive all that you require from this exquisite transmission.

Fírinne blinked slowly, letting her eyes adjust to external light. She wondered for the gazillionth time how humans perceive light in this way when the brain lives in a closed environment. Moonlight glowed silver along the ridgeline of the Continental Divide. Softly echoed along the piece of Selenite she held in her hands, it was enough. Gently placing the stone on the table next to her, she reached for her journal and began to write.

Liquid crystalline structures of embodiment, she wrote. These hold a powerful energy of sustainable nurturing. An adamance of inner guidance. The calm unity, harmony, peace, and power of living as Grace.

"So, what is my heart asking for, deeply yearning for?"

Her Source essence answered through her heart and pen.

Like any other being, you yearn for comfort, security, love, and understanding. Give yourself the gift of these. Now filled with completion, your heart recalls images of what feels like absence. Your awareness is moving into the infinite flow of deep caring that will then move through you and take care of you first. When you are the Source essence, the foundational freedom of flow, all requirements take care of themselves.

Conscious living, the primary theme of this lunation, brings the support of Selenite, its strength and clarity, into the first lunation, which was the Pearl. It brings a new level of purity and higher octaves of light. Each gem brings in the highest octaves of its energy emanations. And all have been infused within the planet Gaia over this past cycle.

The clasp is closing and bringing the cycle full circle so that everything can light up, grow, and be nurtured from within.

This initiation is a deep listening, a deep receiving. You are part of a cresting wave of awakening.

Fírinne sighed, unfolded her legs, and realized she was not thinking. Her mind was still, her ears open to hear. Smiling softly, she turned on her computer, ready to scribe.

"Is your attention so cheaply purchased?" The Matriarch Dragon's voice startled her out of her reverie. "Put the box down and receive.

"Let divine intelligence impulse and guide you. Let it light your way. The first infusion, way back in January, held a key. What was it?"

Fírinne's answer was immediate. "I saw a trinary strand of threads, spiraling like DNA. The linked strands held a very refined gold essence twisting through the year. Then, thirteen gems showed up along the strands. Each stone appeared clouded, so I could not see too far ahead. I knew each gem was present to add to the chain and give its gifts to a sacred circle."

The Matriarch Dragon nodded sagely. Her growled response thrummed through the ethers. "As you self-recognize, something resonates with you and within you. Let it in. Open to it. Receive. Don't reach. Let it flow with you as you.

"Let this be your un-boxing day, a sun/moon cycle in which the roar of your joy floods your body and the planet you live on. What will you do with fully embodied freedom? Anything you choose. The way to move through any portal or gateway is to become its essence. As such an opening radiates through you, as you, all such becomings are moved beyond what was and into what might be possible.

"Your thirteen-moon cycle for the year 2023 is complete. Let yourself receive the gift. Let yourself become it."

"I don't want this to be over," Fírinne almost wailed like a child.

"Over?!" Every teacher or guide she had ever had roared with laughter. She felt even her angel family dissolve into mirth. Dragons rolled with glee in every dimension.

Your real life has only begun.

Epilogue

∞ ∞ ∞

"Is this an epilogue to my story or an epitaph of an old life? Maybe both," Fírinne chuckled. Perhaps it didn't matter.

Barely recognizable as the one who had begun this journey, she sat outdoors on a bench in an open space that provided a clear view of the Continental Divide. Mid-winter cold enveloped her body as though she had fallen into deep water. Frigid air followed her breath, making the little hairs in her nose crisp and crinkle. She coughed once, involuntarily. Warm air from her lungs flooded her nasal passages, soothing her body into stillness.

She had never felt this kind of discomfort in the Himalayas, though those climes were arguably much more frigid. "Perhaps the butter tea had helped;" she grinned as she regretted leaving her thermos behind. "I still love tea," she mused. "That has not changed, anyway."

"No?" The question echoed all around her. The revitalized union of Earth's elements rang with renewed joy. "Look around you. It is time to notice what changes are mirrored to you by your environment, by nature. Your perceptual lenses have altered. You no longer need to be quite so passive in your observations."

Fírinne wrapped a woolen blanket around herself, tucking it beneath her where she sat. She had not brought her journal, as the gloves she wore, though deliciously warm, were too cumbersome for writing.

She wondered about the Observer Function, as she had come to call her ability to perceive the world and its beings through unfiltered eyes.

Joy rushed through her heart in rapturous harmony with the waves of the world. Mountain ranges to the East and West emitted a constant, comforting hum. This all-pervasive sound was not the "Aum" she had been taught to listen for or to practice. It felt like the purring of a contented planet; one stroked into transcendence by Source Herself.

'Stroked into transcendence,' now, there was a phrase. "Always when I don't have my journal," Fírinne chuckled.

"You will remember," thrummed the planet.

Soothed, comforted, envigorated, and enfolded by Divine Love, Gaia hurtled into new emergence. Gone were her old archetypes and funhouse mirrors of support. "Did you have those as well?" Fírinne asked her beloved Gaia.

"What did you think supported yours?" was not the expected answer.

"Really?!" With that, Fírinne's mind boggled. The chestnut saying, 'truth will out' filled her awareness. "Well, it certainly has outed...what, exactly?"

Immersed in Oneness, as 'boots on the ground,' your awareness implodes into Infinity. Your authentic experience of life has just begun.

Pink sunrise glowed on the peaks before her. Geese rose overhead, taking their morning flight towards the sun—each winged body pulsing harmoniously with Gaia, her ley lines, and her new adventures. Pristine magmatic elementals flowed beneath the Earth's crust, joyously singing light codes into being. Fírinne watched these codes as each wove its way upward, creating ripples, currents, and energy waves embraced and integrated by mountains, lakes, seas, and the green world.

Nature burst through Fírinne's vision in all her radiant glory. Life opened itself to her in ways she had always known yet had not fully lived.

"Will wonders never cease?" her literary mind supplied. "Of course not," she thought. "Worlds are built of wonder." She wanted to embrace the mountains as they had embraced her upon arrival. Even as the desire formed, she felt it happen. She was their embodiment of wisdom, strength, and power. She felt their purpose as though it was her own. "This is how life works," she breathed to the dawn.

Memories flooded her awareness. She felt her young body perched on a balcony rail, suspended over the hill's edge behind her bedroom. It had almost been close enough for her to leap into the trees, but not quite. From this vantage point, she could see the wood and, in winter, the creek and fields below.

Then, she was at Font's Point in California, inching to the cliff's edge with the vast desert stretching and shimmering below her. She felt no fear of falling as the land embraced her presence. Time-spinning, her memory shifted to the top of Hag's Head on the West coast of Ireland, legs anchored into the stone against wild winds that offered to sweep her out to sea. Salt air and the scent of magic braced her senses.

Her vision recalled the feeling of life in remote mountain towns and the palpable stillness that sang spirit songs in her heart.

"The heights have held me," she whispered to the wind. "Whether by mountains or waves, all along, I am, I have been, held."

With that, she recognized her presence within the heart of the Matriarch Dragon, the All, and the Infinite.

Was there ever any difference?

Source's voice resounded in deafening silence, like a symphony made of millions.

Fírinne found herself walking. Cold. Movement would help. Her feet knew the way. Her body had always known this way.

Being Love.

Acknowledgements

A year spent scribing for the Source of us all has been another gift, in a lifetime filled with Infinite support.

I could not have made it through the scribing process without the support of dear friends whose dedication to the Source of us all at least equals my own.

I wish to acknowledge Terry Bellamak for her endless cold reads, her sublime ability to nitpick, and to ask questions that make me want to hurl the laptop across the room, but push me to dig deeper in committing clarity to the page.

Bethany Pozzi-Johnson's encouragement and talent for embracing nuances of continuity and vibrancy of story makes her a writing coach worthy of the name.

I would also like to acknowledge Rachel Naples, whose editing skills have helped me to become a better writer. A brilliant writer herself, when Rachel says "It's good," it means the world.

And the excellent assistance of Joan Weisman, without whom my business would not function.

And, of course, my gratitude to the Source of us all, for the privilege of this task. The transmissions in this book are immense, intense, and, perhaps for some, ahead of their linear time sequence. I trust that what the Infinite wished to communicate will be received where and how it is meant to be.

About The Author

Nalini Macnab

Nalini MacNab is an internationally known writer, spiritual guide, and transformational seer. She has spent a lifetime mentoring others in living as a directly aligned, conscious part of the infinite field. Nalini is the author of several books outlining the ins, outs, and adventures of evolving consciousness. She is the founder of the online Galactic Mother Temple, a collaborative community of individuals whose intent is to form a circle of Illumination.